For
My Mum

Audrey Hilda Bradbury
17 August 1925 – 9 June 2017

With love

Man, there's no boundary line to art.

Charlie Parker

In the depth of winter I finally learned that there
was in me an invincible summer.

Albert Camus

The Back End of the Big City
America
Summer
1959

I

The knocking lit his subconscious and ignited a dream. Upon awaking, he would not remember the dream, but would know only that it had seemed to last for hours and that it had left him without hope; depleted and in need of something that did not exist

He pulled his blanket over his head. If he went back into the darkness, perhaps he would be able to re-enter that nether world, to cross that Rubicon and find whatever it was that had left him so utterly drained.

The knocks continued. There was no sign of impatience or urgency to them, just a constant, regular knock; da-*da*, da-*da*, like a heartbeat, lup-dup, lup-dup. He could see in his mind the gloved knuckles strike upon the flaky grey paint of his wooden door, go back an inch, then come down again with all the precision, thoughtlessness and reliability of an automaton. It begged a mix of politeness and determination, of doing what had to be done with the least malevolence and the minimum fuss. Yet he knew that it would not go away. He squeezed his eyes tightly as he would when he was a child and unable to grasp sleep. Those moments stayed. He could feel the same panic build within him now, the same imprisonment, the claustrophobia of entrapment, where one could neither find symbiosis with the trap nor break away from it. Surviving all traps was about symbiosis. One could survive anything if one was willing to compromise.

What did he dream? He could feel the puffy, sleep-swelled flesh around his eyes as he sought to extinguish his senses. This had happened a thousand times before, the emergence into sunlight to mourn the loss of his cocoon, but this time, it mattered, it mattered because it could take him away from the gloved hand that had brought down the gavel and passed sentence upon him. But one could not exist without the other. The despair at his lost dream would not have existed without the cancerous knock and the knock would, without the dream, be no more than a knock.

Now it was all. Now it was his prison, his trap, his claustrophobia, his fear. No childish eyes would save him now. No blanket smothering him like an overprotective mother would keep reality at bay. He felt watery fury seep from his eyes as he opened them. He could smell his night time breath as it cloyed upon the filthy blanket. He was rotten within, he knew it. Sleep allowed the rot to crawl from his belly. Light passed through the time-thawed weave of the blanket and flecked his grey sheet. The warmth of his filthy breath stole the air and forced his head into the open. He gulped like a man breaking the meniscus, his moist eyes wide and wild, his forehead as knotted as the bark of a tree.

He filled his lungs. His eyes swivelled towards the door. They were filled with cow-like fear, suffused by diamonds of impatience. He cursed. How dare they? How dare they rap their velvet knuckles against his only defence against the world. They were boulders slung by the trebuchet against his castle walls. He could give into this intimidation and allow the enemy within, in the hope that they were no more enemy than birds passing overhead. Or he could withstand the siege, live upon his own flesh, quench his thirst with his own urine. He could recycle himself in order to survive. Would it be possible to survive self-absorption? No, it was absurd. His hunger would survive his body's ability to heal. His urine would eventually turn to syrup and turn against the machine that produced it. His body would run rampant with the poisons it had rejected in the first place.

There was nothing for it but to look for truce. So long as the boulder fell against the curtain walls, he would never get any peace and he would always wonder who it was that had caused him to poison himself. To die was bad enough, but to die in ignorance was inexcusable.

'Wait.'

His own voice startled him. It was heavy with stale breath and sticky saliva. His dry throat grazed the air with a diabolical edge. Good. Perhaps it would drive them away. Perhaps he had found the antidote to the slingshot, a fearsome retort, but he regretted it immediately, aware that, if whoever it was left, then he would never know who had tried to storm his citadel.

'Wait.'

Softer this time. There was pleading in his tone. He was happy with himself. To produce pleading on demand was a well-honed skill. This might have been too much. He felt a pang of shame at his retreat, his surrender, his willingness to capitulate, his need. He had no propensity for propinquity and yet all he could feel was a panicked regret.

He threw the blanket to the floor and exposed his naked body. It was greased by a sheen of sweat. The perspiration pooled in the creases of his abdomen. He held his breath and watched each suicidal drop jump with every throb of his aorta. With each breath it rolled off the side of his belly and onto the thundercloud of sheet, where it gathered like a storm waiting to erupt across his silent room. He repulsed himself. He was the only guilty party in the room. Only he had subdued his shadows and forced them to fight for life with the light. Only he had suffocated the child as it lay innocently sleeping, only to awaken at the smothering and die in the darkness of age.

Yet there was within this turmoil a certain satisfaction, that he had been right all along, that he had seen the future and shed the past. He had become what he most feared. In this, he was absolved. To fulfil your destiny, to foresee the binding of your soul, took greatness, took mastery. This was not fate and he doubted the existence of destiny, he simply believed in the fragile psychology of humankind. That was perhaps the only place for fate in the scheme, the shredding of a man from the wholeness of youth to the worn remnants of threadbare age. He accepted his decay with grace in the same way that one accepted the long-expected assassin and the coldness of the grave. One could not avoid the inevitable, so he had embraced it, from an early age, had lived it and slipped knowingly towards the abyss, in the same way the captain of a crippled boat steered straight and true towards the waterfall, no hope of touching land, only the determination to reach the drop with his hand upon the wheel. Once one accepted the flow, then all one had to do was go with it.

The knocking continued. He pulled himself to the edge of the bed and looked for his clothes. They were out of reach. He had taken them off the night before and, in his anaesthetised state, simply deposited them in the same place where he had made the decision to finally sleep, without thought of the consequences. He wasn't the kind of drunk to fall asleep where he fell. He was too practised for that, and too fussy. He needed comfort to sleep, safety, the scent of his own dirt, the coolness of his own musty pillow. So he threw off his clothes and stranded them like a snake did its skin.

Now, they were too far away, out of arm's length and beyond a stride, so he stooped and picked up his damp charcoal blanket, wrapped it around his shoulders and wandered, heavy-footed with sleep, towards the door. His thighs shook as he stood. They were, unlike his belly, thin and without stamina. The slightest effort sent them into an uncontrolled quiver. He could barely feel the soles of his feet against the floor. He walked as if on cotton wool, uncertain of the steadiness of his ship, of the reliability of the boards beneath him. If he had had the ability to step outside of himself and see himself as he was, he would have been tempted to laugh, for he imagined himself as a fat flamingo upon sticks for legs which lifted its feet clear of the water with each step as if uncertain as to where they were unless he could see them. He was, however, without the flamingo's balletic grace, as if those thin, elegant toes had been substituted by the stumps of a rhino, not built to step lightly, but to shake the very earth as it walked.

He could not remember the last time someone other than his landlady had come to his door. She only came for the rent or to ensure that he was still alive. He understood that. There was uncertainty in his survival and she had a business to run. He was a temporary asset. She needed to make sure that the asset lived, not in the sense of having any responsibility towards the asset, only in the sense that it was alive. It lives, I live, they live, we live. When he had moved into the bedsit, she had told him that one of her previous tenants, in this very room, had lain dead for a week. She had been forced to climb the stairs for her income. She had knocked with fair firmness at the door, but there had been no reply. She had called his name, without malice or song. She had not seen him leave, not for some time so knew he was in. After knocking again, still to no avail, she had become convinced that he was merely trying to avoid payment believing, as many did, that silence lent invisibility, that a lack of sound forced people to dismiss you from their minds, no matter the facts. In many cases, she thought, this was true, but never when money was involved. You might forget the face of your dead husband or wife, but never the face of a debtor. There was none of the comfort in debt that there was in blood and there wasn't, she was certain, much comfort in blood. Sanguineous proximity was no guarantee of correctitude, as she liked to say. Anyway, people faded through comfortable affection, all that was left were the rags and bones of memory, nothing substantial. Debtors lived on in discomfort, like poltergeists, rattling the owed pennies like chains, perhaps because we were more dependent of our debtors than the beloved deceased. There was always consequence to debt, for all concerned. His concerns, however, were not her concerns. She had made that mistake once, a long time ago, when she had inclined towards lenience with a tenant. She had possessed a better nature back then, along with softer skin and a kinder heart. Not only had he not paid her, he had made delicious and unbounded love to her and then stolen her valuables when she fell into an unarousable post-coital sleep.

Anyway, she had used a skeleton key to enter the room ('I had knocked and knocked *and knocked*', she felt obliged to say). It was winter and the room was like an icebox. This was probably what had preserved the body so well. The window was open and snowflakes had drifted in and settled upon the frost. If only, she had said a little too regretfully, it had been two months earlier. But for that body it would have been quite festive. She hoped that he had no objection moving into what had once been the room of a dead man. He had said no, that it didn't bother him. The streets were full of dead men. In a world of three billion people, it would be difficult to stand in a place where someone had not died. If it bothered him, he would be forever rooted to a single spot awaiting his own death.

Anyway, that was why she climbed the stairs to claim the rent. A dead body was an inconvenience, and not just financially. The police had chewed on that death like mad dogs, determined that some sort of foul play had been involved. In the end, in the absence of evidence and in the inconvenient presence of truth (a large river of blood that had risen from ruptured varices in the lower oesophagus and trickled back into the lungs), they had relented. In future, if she could make sure of catching them just before they lurched over the precipice, then she could ship them off to hospital and let it be their problem. Leave the body on a neighbour's doorstep. It was a good rule in life.

He admired her practicality, but he didn't actually like the woman. She looked like his grandfather and he could not look favourably upon any woman who looked like his grandfather. He had been a bitter old bastard, even to his last breath.

He knew anyway that it was not her at the door. It was not rent time. Despite everything, he was not behind on the rent. In fact, he owed money to no one. That and his rightness about the inevitability of his decline gave him some pride. It wasn't her knock either. She had the knock of a bag of bones, all sharp-edged, without resonance. Her knock could have been the knock of Death itself; steady, relentless and without the warmth of flesh. He could tell that these fingers were gloved; the material deadened the sound. He could also tell that the man, for it was a man, he could tell by the weight behind it, was not of slender build, might even have tended towards the portly, towards the edge of gout. The constancy of his knock suggested that he was a man unlikely to give up, who was used to getting his own way, and getting your own way could be guaranteed by only two methods; wealth or criminality. That didn't of course mean that the two were exclusive of each other. He had known many wealthy criminals and many wealthy men who tended towards criminality, either because they needed to do so to maintain or increase their wealth or because one day they suddenly found themselves unencumbered by the boundaries of ordinary men, immune to the law. They were however, two distinct beings. He had also known poor criminals, because through either laziness, a lack of greed or poor luck they never quite achieved the riches they wanted. Criminality for criminals was a way of life, a job, something that flowed through their veins and the only way they knew to survive. In the wealthy, it was a by-product, like the sulphurous smoke of the coal burned in industry at the height of the Industrial Revolution and through the poisonous air of the fifties, a necessary evil. If one wanted light and warmth, one had to compromise. And he was realistic enough to understand the weaknesses of a man. If a man was not to be tempted, then temptation should not exist. The thirsty man drank, the hungry man ate. One could not blame him for that. It did not make him a gourmet or a drunk, merely a man. Man was fragile. Man was easily broken. Man did not have to fall far for the cracks to appear.

Neither did a criminal have any business knocking at his door, not when there was a perfectly serviceable window available, and no one would come to his door with a gun in their hand and intent in their soul, not in this part of town. The lock on the door could have been picked by a two year old with a hair pin and an ounce of patience. No, there were easier ways to rob a man. He had no social or business dealings with criminals either, so he dismissed that idea.

This left only the wealthy man. He realised that, by assuming the wealth of the individual, he dismissed the honest poor and the bourgeoisie, but he was even less likely to have dealings with them than the others. There was no place in his life for the ordinary and, in among the ordinary, he could include friends. He had no friends, but this was rarely a basis for regret. He had tried friends, in the same way that he had tried marijuana, but neither had suited him. He, quite simply, did not believe in friendship. It was just not a workable concept. The idea of true friendship was a lofty and unattainable notion achievable only by the weak, the deluded and the easily led. He believed in symbiosis, the beneficial collusion of two entities, but that there could be any more to friendship than need or greed, self-aggrandisement or vanity, was an idea with which he would have no truck. Each one of us, king, queen or common man, lived to serve himself. When it came down to it, people were animals and animals did not have friends, not if they were to survive. Even those that hunted in packs broke up into individuals once the prey was down; then it was each man for himself. Hierarchy reinforced this, the alpha male, the subservient pup who would eventually challenge that male to the death, and it was no different in mankind. Any animal that broke from this was cast out if it could not bite and claw its way to the top. Any human to deviate from these rules was imprisoned or executed or shunned. The only difference between humans and animals was that humans knew what they were doing. They were consciously oppressive. All kings were sociopaths.

He turned the key in the lock and, as the inner workings of the aged lock slid stiffly from their moorings, the knocking ceased.

Panic jolted him violently. He tore open the door, his eyes round with pleading and expectation, his teeth bared between rictus and smile. He no longer knew how to form a face. There was nobody. He hugged the blanket to himself, felt its now cool clamminess envelop him like the dead skin of another and stepped out of the room.

A single skylight, covered by moss and dust, lit the hall and stairway. The light fell in copper green as it seeped weakly through. He lurched towards the banister and craned over. The blanket slid moistly from his shoulders and fell to the ground, leaving him naked in a single piercing shaft of golden light that squeezed between the clumps of moss on the filthy glass. He listened for footsteps, for breathing, but there was none. Nausea overwhelmed him as he fell to his knees and peered between the balusters. He wanted to cry, but would not let himself do so. So hungry had he been for this morsel of companionship that he had tried to deny himself the pleasure and, now that it was gone, he was filled with remorse. He loathed himself for the disgust he felt for his fellow humans. He longed to feel the compassion that he perceived others felt, though he believed them all disingenuous, but he could not. He had never been able to do so and had spent his life searching for that moment within him that he knew existed somewhere and put it upon canvas. It was the only way he knew. There was nothing real in his work, only longing. The spots of paint upon the floor were the only genuine parts of his expression, the only uncontrived spontaneity.

Now that same longing sat naked upon the landing and clung to the darkness below in the hope of being extinguished.

2

The windowsill was wide enough to accommodate one, two at a push. The sash window, bitten wretched by time and the elements, lent a fine view upon the streets below which had once served as an inspirational spectacle. Each pane of glass now had its own dusty halo, occasionally strippled by rain, through which he could stare at the world in a misty bokeh and imagine each passer-by caught for that moment in that pose and each pose would in itself tell a tale, from a purposeful stride or a lazy amble, to the bitter knitted brow or faraway eyes that took them some place tolerable for a bent moment in time. The inspiration, he knew, was still in there, somewhere, he had just lost the willingness to look for it. He was caught in a purgatory where he took complete joy in everything he saw, but he could do nothing about it. It had become forbidden fruit and to even look at the fruit was tantamount to self-betrayal. He did not want the connection, but he could not help himself, in the same way that someone who cut themselves committed the act just to see if they could feel pain any more, to confirm their humanity, to show themselves that they were still alive. He longed for the connection, but despised it and feared it, for he knew that nothing could come of it but harm.

Now, in the heat of this glorious summer, he opened the sash window and the sounds of traffic, the throaty blasts of motorcycles, the protestations of double-clutches, the squeal of dusty brakes, rose in a synaesthetic union and coloured the air. Individuals could not be heard above the noise, but their lips moved, a silent jibber-jabber that contorted their mouths and puffed their cheeks and flared their nostrils like racehorses stretching for the final post. Their heads bobbed and shook like cheap advertising gimmicks on the dashboard, while their hands kneaded the air to help them sculpt their thoughts into words. Those on their own were barely present, their faraway eyes betraying lies of distant shores and happy homes and the contentment felt in the simple task of mowing the lawn. They had compromise on their minds. Almost anything was better than the something towards which they travelled. It was better to lose a finger than an arm, a toe rather than a leg. It was better to hang wallpaper on a sunny summer day than march in blind unison to the mechanical beats of the new human heart.

He had tried, more than once. He had tried to become a part of the salmon flow, had even grown to like the calming stroke of the current against his back, but it had never taken long for him to realise that what he was heading for was the shallows, the final dump of his fertility upon a stranger's eggs and an exhausted, shabby death in an unflowing trap of familiarity. Was it possible to despise and envy all those who passed below in their own small Hell? Was it right? Did he have the right to despise their passivity in the face of such overwhelming inevitability or envy their ability to do so without screaming? It was actually he who was screaming. It was he who was feeling the pain. It was he, through choice, who fought, embraced and feared the end. Those people, those ants, who followed their scent day after day after day without question or pause, had no idea of their enormous obligation to life. He wished that he was one of them, able to walk around the obstacles set before them instead of trying to clamber over them or tear them apart, as he had always done.

But they were all going to that same end, whatever the method. They were brothers and sisters, sons and daughters of Adam and Eve, who would all end up in solitude. The journey, in the end, was irrelevant. There was no point travelling hopefully when one was bound by nature to arrive.

He poured the remnants of yesterday's wine into a tumbler laced at the base with wine jam, that sweet concoction of leftovers that stayed in the bottom of a glass, no matter how you tried to suck it dry. After several days, it became semi solid and sweeter and added to the new pourings. He had long ago given up the pretence of using a proper glass. He was pleased to see that the leftovers came to the lip of the glass. He squeezed *la dernière goutte* from the bottle and craned his neck to the glass to avoid the risk of spillage. With pursed lips, he sucked at the contents. He closed his eyes and waited. Slowly (and more slowly each day), he felt the wine spread through him like rhizomes and make him whole again. It was a guilty relief to feel the sensation. He had tried to do without, but he was weak and would feel himself begin to fracture with each unanaesthetised second that passed.

He put the glass down firmly, next to the window frame where it was less likely to be knocked and bleed, and lowered himself from the sill.

The studio - it had been advertised as such – had appealed to him, not least because of the name. It was a bed-sitter, actually a room, that was all, but to advertise it as she did had been a mistress-stroke on the part of the landlady, especially in this part of town. It was a room, merely a room. A box of accoutrements, one of them being him.

In the far corner, next to his easel, his small table of paints and brushes, his canvases, jam jars full of cloudy water and spit-spotted rags, was his turntable. It was a red Dansette Conquest, with a cream lid. It reminded him of the advertisements he saw in magazines for finned Chevy Bel Airs, '51 De

Sotos and Plymouths, that weren't just cars, but were passports to different dimensions; otherworldly, science fiction flyers. The Dansette represented the same freedom. It was a vortex to that other dimension, an escape, a place where he too could wander with faraway eyes and listen with admiration and envy to the wonders of creation.

Vivaldi, Albinoni and Bird had become the sound of his captivity, the soundtrack to his life. Their sweet sorrow broke his heart, that irresistible urge, awoke the passions in him. They had come to control him, to dictate his moods, his brushstrokes, his subjects, his eating and drinking, his happiness and despair. They made him want to live and content to die. They filled him with envy and the affirmation of a wasted life. They gave him hope, a breeze in the Doldrums, that there might yet be further to go, discoveries to be made. Then winter set in and he realised that he too was at season's end and at the whim of men long since dead or distant enough to be not just dead, but non-existent. He envied and despised them for their power. He loved them for their caress. They brought him relief in his hopelessness and fear in the hope.

He flicked through his collection and plucked *One Night in Birdland* out from the pack. He removed the heavy vinyl from its sleeve. His eyes held the cover as he did so, the oh-so-cool purple pinstripe and the sax, ready to tear things apart and then put them gently back together. Fats Navarro, on trumpet, would be dead a week after recording it. Did he know? Did he know that he was entering the last week of his life? That this would be the last thing he laid down for the world?

His fingers touched only the label in the centre of the disc while his eyes followed that single groove from beginning to end. Deftly, he moved the record to between his palms and then laid it out on the turntable. He tweezered the arm between his fingers and laid the diamond life-giver upon the vinyl. It scratched the air like an incoming message with an outer space urgency, then in came *Wahoo* through the thin speaker at the front of the Dansette and carried him away.

He closed the lid, running his fingers over the patina of paint flicks that had settled on it. It felt real. It was uncontrived, unrehearsed. He had often wondered if he would be better off just spilling and spraying his work, like that crazy Pollock, but with less intent. At least it would be more honest than what he turned out now. Everything went through the processor before being laid tritely upon the canvas. The closest that he ever came to honesty was that he never sketched, not unless poor memory demanded it, never went over and over the finest detail. But what came out, after being processed in his mind, then his heart, his gut, then finally his fingers, was still processed, still contrived, still an arrival at an interpretation of his perception and, as such, it was dishonest. At least Pollock, for all his meticulously placed dribblings, came closer to the spontaneity that a real artist should have. It didn't matter if it was pictures or words, pencil or paint, poetry or portrait, the first emissions were the ones that mattered, for they were the ones that fathered the honest child. It didn't have to make sense, it just had to mean, to have purpose, to speak.

He was lucky though, luckier than many. At least he had, by hook and crook, managed to get by. He had combined the tyrant commercialism with his real needs and managed to keep his head above water. So long as he was able to lift a brush, he would be able to pay his rent. If he could no longer lift a brush, there would be no point paying his rent. No point. If he thought about it for too long, he would slip into broody melancholia, make him want to break his brushes and shred his canvasses. All the work that had brought him reward had been done for others. The work he did for himself made next to nothing, so he constantly had to block from his mind the knowledge that the next stroke upon the canvas was for another, never for him. Of course, they were done for pennies too but, in the end, the pennies also went to somebody else. It didn't stop him doing his work, for he loved it, every moment, every smell that fell onto his tongue so that he could taste it, every line and curve and mix, and it tasted like creation. The circularity of the whole cycle made him afraid that he had become caught in the trap that he had always consciously tried to avoid. He suspected that his failure to remain in gainful employment, whatever that meant, was due to his desire to remain free of the trap. In the end he chewed his metaphysical leg off to get free. He always found a way to corrupt the goodness to be found in a decent, a 'proper', job. If he could put the blame for his failure on somebody else, then so much the better. He had always been reluctant to take responsibility for his life and using others to carry the burden of blame relieved him of that.

He took a lingering look at the blank canvas that lay like snow upon the deciduous easel and tried hard to imagine what could be on there. There was little that inspired him anymore. For that reason alone, he was glad of the commercial work. For someone like him, advertising represented a poor challenge. The ideas were already there; the subject matter, the target audience, the medium, the desires of the client. If he was honest, he would have told them that any precocious six-year-old with a modicum of talent and an only slightly withered arm could do what he did, but he saw no reason to give a six-year-old a leg up – the competition was hard enough; they would soon be stealing the food from his plate.

His most recent commission (it had to be called a commission for the sake of decency) was for a small yet flourishing business in the oil industry. It was all family and teeth and smiles and trees and the saccharine delights of nature and man coming together as one to make the world a better place, never mind the fact that man was slowly strangling the life out of nature with the by-products of nature's compressed, fossilised delights. But he knew that he had better make the most of the work that came his way. Nowadays it was all going to agencies, those white-shirted busy bees that hid in their towering concrete hives. People like him, the independents, would be forced to shut up shop and fly obediently into those hives and produce the pre-ordered honey that Queen Money demanded. Independent thought was dying as surely as the earth itself. Damn humanity, he thought. We fuck everything up. If we had to fuck up to stay alive, we'd fuck that up too.

He waved a hand dismissively at the canvas. It would come. It always did. It was just a part of the process, to put himself through torture before he puked it all out in one feverish sitting.

He stopped at his bedside table, which wasn't really that at all, more of an accidental cupboard, on the way back to his perch at the window, and picked up his cigarettes. He smoked Chesterfields. He smoked Chesterfields because he had always smoked Chesterfields and that was that. He had once tried a Marlboro and nearly shit himself he coughed so hard, so Chesterfields it was. He lit it and inhaled deeply, then went back to the windowsill and stretched out his legs once more.

The sun, already racing up the cobalt blue sky, had heated the sill up to boiling point. The glass in the windows, despite the dirt, magnified the heat a hundred times as it seared through the top half of the sash. Now it massaged his shoulder and the side of his face. He could feel his skin tighten. He put his hand down and found his tumbler of wine without even looking. He took a large sip and allowed it to mingle with the nicotine in his veins and bring him pleasantly to the edge of early day nausea. Sweet, sweet, he mused. Sweet, sweet.

Below him, summer was in full swing. He could smell hot concrete and electricity and singed petrol. Despite the sombre veil of work and business, which cloaked all in a weary grey, there were splashes of colour, corn yellow and red and sky blue and lime green and brilliant white, that wonderful rainbow that winter throttled in the stifling rigidity of overcoats. Skirts and dresses swished and twirled, high heels and low shoulders clicked and rolled and cars ticked-tacked soft tyres against gluey tarmac with windows down and bare arms surfing the air. A thousand radios played a thousand songs so that all the sounds of industry mingled with all the bebop trumpets and all the vagabond drums to create a new panegyric on mankind. Behind him and around him the Bird flew free and skimmed upon the myriad notes as if on a rise of warm air.

From here it all looked so fine, so full of promise. His eyes fell upon a girl in a summer dress. It was white with flowers of dark purple and red and leaves of dark green that threaded through the flowers on sinuous vines. The dress formed an oval around her neck so that her neck and half her shoulders were exposed. Around her waist she had a thin black belt that accentuated the perfect triangle of her torso so that, beneath her waist, the dress blossomed and took on a life of its own with each step she took. Her shoes were black slip-ons with no heel. She walked like a ballerina, all balls of the feet and barely touching the ground. Her hair was short and blonde, her skin pale, but a healthy pale. He couldn't see for sure, but he imagined her eyes to be a brilliant blue so that they stood out like blue diamonds against her pale skin. Her lips wore red lipstick and were thick, kissable lips. Her nose had the slightly upturned impudence of an imp. It was delightful. She was delightful.

He loved her. At that moment he loved her and wanted to fall to his knees before her, his head against her warm belly, her hand in his hair. She was the most beautiful woman on that urban canvas. She stood out like a goddess among mortals, seemed to shine against the dullness of the ordinary. If she was here now, before him, he would simply stare and take in each perfect molecule of her being. He would kiss her full red lips and feel their warmth and their pillow softness against his own lips. He would kiss her neck and take in her scent, the natural musk and the talcum and the refreshing hint of lemon that he knew would be in the mix somewhere. When he was ready, when he had paid homage to this goddess, he would undress her, slowly, then lay her down upon his grey bed and make love to her as no man was capable of making love but in his dreams.

He loved her with all his soul. He loved her.

But he knew that it would not last. Love could not last. He had learned that love was an unattainable concept. He knew that, as soon as she uttered a sound, the goddess would descend to the human condition. From her mouth would fall opinion, dogma and the spittle of righteous prejudice with which he would quickly grow weary. Her body would be like any other, rampant with odour and decay and he would be left with little more than the prospect of her going the same way as all. The zenith of their love was now, when they did not know each other, when they had not tasted each other's sour breath, when the thing that bonded them was their distance. With his thoughts, love fell from its height and plummeted to a messy death. He watched her go and felt utter, depthless sadness. He had met her, fallen in love, fallen out of love and watched her die in the time it took her feet to dance between the chrome and skip upon the kerb at the other side of the road.

He drained the rest of his wine. It would not be enough, not for a man as in love as he. He admitted to himself in the silence of his own confessional that he loved her. Her image was imprinted, burned, into his brain. She was and would remain, ideal. Still, he had more wine, that was the important thing. He would drink it over the course of the day until, by twilight, he would be numb enough to slough his skin again and sleep.

He took one long final drag upon his cigarette until he could feel the heat between his fingers, then crushed it into an ashtray replete with the corpses of the previous day.

God, he thought as he watched the girl turn a corner and disappear from his life forever. God, how I love you.

Then there was a knock at the door.

3

He felt the chambers of his heart collide. Even above the Dansette the knock could be heard and its double drum caused the music to fall apart in an arrhythmia of missed beats, to disintegrate into a meaningless, jarring cacophony. The moment of delight that he had passed was past.

He reached for his tumbler and realised to his horror that it was empty. Instead, he took out a cigarette, his eyes all the time upon the back of the door, and lit it. He could not now pretend that he was not in, not with the Bird loose. The caller would have had to have been deaf to have failed to hear it. He lowered his legs and sat hunched upon the edge of the sill, the sun hot upon his back, his hands folded over the edge of the sill, his knuckles white.

The knocks persisted in the same relentless fashion as they had before. Despite the music, they never dropped a beat. He was able to count the time between them; one-two, pause-knock, one-two, pause-knock, one-two...

This was punishment, he thought, for his thoughts about the girl. He had sinned, had lecherous thoughts and a moment of insane hope and now reality was here to punish him. Why would the world, that wheezing lung, not leave him alone?

He pushed himself up and stood limply, his arms flaccid at his sides, an octopus on the dry Greek dock, his hands no more use than weighty tentacles spread out like Gorgon hair, his shoulders round, his head bowed and mouth agape. Only his eyes remained levelled at the door like the eyes of the insane upon the nothing that was there. This would be his last chance, he knew this. If he failed to heed the call this time, then it would be gone forever. Whoever it was showed persistence, persistence and need. Rarely had anybody ever shown a persistent need for the occupant of this box.

He launched himself towards the door, his cigarette between his lips, and pressed his ear to the back of it.

Lup-dup, lup-dup.

Should he open it? Should he speak? He had almost begged them to wait when they had called before, but they had nonetheless gone. They might not have heard his pathetic pleading of course. His throat had been gritty with the night's dryness, his vocal cords brittle, unable to break free from the sooty cancerous deposits of the previous day's three dozen cigarettes. To himself, he had sounded loud, he had been the only sound, but to a stranger he might have sounded like a distant motorbike or the house waking in the hot new sun or maybe he made no sound at all. More likely he had made no sound at all, which was why they had left.

Upon impulse, in a single, swift, war-like moment of courage, he grabbed the handle and opened the door. He was afraid that there would be no one there again, that in the split second he had made the decision to open the door, that they would be gone, down the stairs and into the chartreuse shadows of the mossy skylight, out into the street to disappear, along with his goddess, around a corner, forever.

He was greeted by a large shadow, faceless, its features lost in the brilliant shaft of light that squeezed between the moss and fell brightly behind them. Their gloved hand was raised to knock again and now hung upon the air unfulfilled.

'Ah,' said the shadow. 'There you are. I was afraid I had had another wasted journey.' There was a pause during which neither man spoke nor moved. 'Invite me in then,' said the shadow. 'I have business.'

The room's occupant stood aside and the large man brushed past. He was made larger by a thick overcoat and fedora hat. All the same, it was clear that, even without these, he would have been a big man. In the light from the window, his features became clear. Despite the extraordinary heat and his thick coat, hat and gloves, he was not sweating. This was made even more surprising by the fact that, as a consequence of sustained and undisguised self-indulgence, he was corpulent. This corpulence overflowed into a neck barely confined by the tight boundaries of a crisp white shirt and then further by a set of jowls that hung like turkey wattles. Yet, for all his self-abuse, he had the smoothest, softest and whitest skin that his host had ever seen. He longed to stretch out a hand and run the backs of his fingers across the visitor's face. The man was without age. Indeed, if a person's history was to be seen upon their brow or around their eyes or in the troughs around their mouths, then this man must have been newborn, for even his eyes, which sat like emeralds beneath two immaculate eyebrows, were unstained by life. The emeralds were embedded in porcelain – white sclera, unblemished by event or disease.

The man removed his gloves, then his hat with fat fingers, the nails embedded like chubby babies and buffed to a shine and, when he found nowhere to place it, he put the gloves inside the hat and handed them to his host. It was put in the only paint-free, stain-free place – the windowsill. The man did the same with his coat. Beneath that he wore a pinstriped blue wool suit with a navy knitted wool tie. His hair, it turned out, was the biggest surprise of all. There was none. It was, with the lack of hair and absence of lines upon his face, as if he was somehow incomplete, as if his creator had become bored and released him into the world in a semi-foetal state. That he seemed physically unaffected by the heat added to his surreal aura. He smelled of citrus and cloves, with an unidentifiable sweetness permeating them. The effect was a little nauseous and yet strangely refreshing and almost festive.

The visitor cast his eyes about the room. He let slip no opinion about it, but his eyes lingered first upon the grey sea of bed and then upon the work area; the easel, the paints, the palettes, the brushes, the speckled Dansette.

Despite the noise that eddied about them, seeping from the streets and leaping from the record player, the frozen air between the two men laid a frosty pall upon the air. The host longed for the stranger to speak again or for himself to find something useful to contribute to the emptiness.

Instead, he fled to his almost cupboard next to his bed and removed an unopened bottle of wine. With what he considered admirable restraint, he removed a pocket knife from his trousers, opened a corkscrew attachment, twisted the corkscrew dead centre into the cork and slowly removed it. There were several reasons for his economy of speed; he wanted to appear to have at least some control but, more importantly, he had learned that any haste in the uncorking of inexpensive wine more often than not led to disappointment and a bottle full of corky sediment. The wine he drank was not of a high standard to begin with, but that was no reason to pollute it further. He felt himself reach for his tumbler with an urgency that was difficult to resist. He knew that once he had supped his medication and taken a few drags on a Chesterfield, he would be ready to confront the invader.

'I'm sorry,' he said, realising his rudeness. 'May I offer you some wine? Or tea? I have some tea...somewhere...I'm sure...'

'No.' The reply came with no intonation whatsoever. It was simply a statement of fact.

'Cigarette?'

'You are the artist, Jumeau?'

'I am,' said Jumeau. 'I am Jumeau. Of course. I am an artist, one of many in this area. We gather like pigeons in the hope of crumbs.' He smiled weakly.

The man's fat lips failed to respond in kind. 'I'll take that as a yes. I am Wint. I want you to paint me.'

'Really?' Jumeau wavered between surprise and disbelief. It occurred to him that the man might be mocking him; one could trip over an artist in this district by simply stepping into the street and dropping a dime. They were indeed more common than the sooted pigeons that gathered on ledges and stalked the sidewalks in search of popcorn and hotdog remnants and were probably considered to be more of a pest. However, several flights of dark and rotten stairs in the less salubrious side of town were quite a risk for a simple mocking. Jumeau dismissed the idea.

It did however occur to him that, desperate as he was, he should at least play slightly hard to get. 'I do have other work. I have a commission.'

Wint looked at the blank canvas that lurked in the shadows. 'Unstarted, I believe.'

'All the same...'

'I'll pay you ten thousand dollars.'

'Ten thousand dollars!'

'I assume that would be sufficient. If you wish to quibble...' Wint showed a first sign of impatience, of any sort of reaction. He closed his lips tightly and sighed. 'I am not a quibbler, but I understand the need in some to negotiate. How much do you want?'

Jumeau took a gulp of wine and lit the cigarette that had been sitting between his fingers for some time. His hands shook and the flame of the match danced seductively before succumbing to the cigarette's lust.

'No more,' he said. He sat down on the windowsill. 'I have never been paid that much to paint anything or anyone. It's not about negotiation.'

Wint huffed derisively through his nose. 'Of course it is. Everything is about negotiation, from getting out of bed in the morning to returning there at night. One rises because the prospect of rising offers more than the prospect of staying in bed. One returns to bed because the benefits of doing so outweigh the benefits of not doing so.' He stood next to Jumeau and peered upon the busy streets. 'Down there,' he said, pointing a pudgy finger, 'everything is by negotiation. It is only when one fails to do so that someone gets run over or stabbed or throws himself in despair from a tenth floor window, but even those apparent acts of carelessness have in some way required a second of negotiation.' He put his hands in his pockets and leaned further towards the window. He could have been a teacher impatiently explaining the rudimentaries of Latin to a class of fools. 'The decision not to look both ways when crossing the road, the decision that gives the mugger permission to use his knife, the moment when life itself becomes the enemy instead of the friend and there is no choice in the end but a quick divorce, are all decisive, however fleeting. The only things that are not by negotiation are birth and death, in the natural course of things. We have no say in either. That is why sometimes people commit suicide, in the mistaken belief that by doing so they have some control. It is, I grant you, a rather one-sided negotiation, but it is nonetheless a conclusion arrived at only after weighing up the pros and the cons and is not a sound counterargument to the stresses of life. They forget that they are merely relinquishing control.' He suddenly turned his deep-green eyes towards his host. 'So, how much do you want?'

Jumeau stared back at Wint and wondered how such a diatribe could possibly commence without alcohol or even before noon. 'Ten thousand dollars is more than enough.'

'You'll accept less then?'

Jumeau laughed. He turned towards the street, unable to hold Wint's gaze any longer. 'I would have done it for half a dozen bottles of cheap red wine before opening the door to you, Mr Wint.'

'Then we will both gain a victory from these negotiations. I will have my painting and you will have enough money to purchase a small vineyard in California, should you wish. Are we agreed?'

'Would you allow me to complete my commission beforehand?'

'Why should I?'

He turned back towards Wint. He had to hold his stony gaze. He had to. He knew he was weak, he knew that he was a cripple who leaned upon the crutch of alcohol to limp through the day, but this mattered. Not much, that was true, but it was the first thing that had mattered for a long time, so that kind of ramped it up, in his eyes at least. 'Because,' he said as firmly as he could, 'I have made a commitment to them. I may be a drunk, but I'm a drunk with standards. What do you say?'

Wint considered. Jumeau knew he was considering because he stopped moving. When Wint had nothing to say, he noticed, he became almost statuesque. He listened without reaction. He thought without expression. It was as if he turned himself off when he wasn't directly involved in the conversation or when there was no conversation to be had. It was simply impossible to tell what was going on within him. His face was apparently incapable of expression (hence no lines). It was only his eyes, those gems, which gave him away. As the machine inside the man whirred and spewed out whatever the bodily equivalent of computer punch cards was, they became wide, more focussed, like a bird of prey zeroing in upon a rodent in the grass fifty feet below. 'How long do you need?'

'Three days, maybe four.'

'How much do they pay you for these three, maybe four, days' work?' Wint anticipated his host's reaction and held up a finger. 'Don't be afraid to be honest with me.'

'I'm not afraid to be honest,' countered Jumeau. 'I'm not sure that it is any of your business, that's all. Just because you have money to throw away does not mean that others have the same lack of regard for it as you.'

'You are wrong, sir. I hold money in very high regard. I know its value exactly. I know what it buys and at what price, and everybody has a price.'

'I don't think that's true.' Jumeau felt a little aggrieved by the covert accusation that he too had a price, could be bought, but this was probably because he knew it to be true.

'Of course it's true!' For the first time since his arrival, Wint became animated. His body language did not change, his hands remained in his pockets, his eyes upon his prey, but for the first time, his voice wavered. 'If I were to bring you a suitcase of cash, enough that you would find it uncomfortable, I could get you to do anything, from killing a child to a homosexual act. None of us thinks that we would break under torture, none of us believes, really *believes*, that he will die. None of us believes that they have a price, that they can be compromised, bought, whored. There is always a line to be crossed at a certain cost.'

'I'm not sure that I agree with you.'

'Because you have not yet reached that lowly place where those things become permissible to you, at least, so you believe. An empty belly is a great incentive to shift the boundaries. Why would a woman become a prostitute if it were not for those desperate needs which could not be met by other means? She allows a man whom she has never met before to enter her privates, to ejaculate upon her, to do unspeakable things to her that she would not even permit a husband to do, so that she might eat. She risks disease, she risks degradation, she risks harm, maybe even murder, to put food in her belly and a roof over her head. Some men travel the world killing other men for a fee. The mercenary might well have different boundaries and a different price to the whore, but they still have a price. Their cost is comparable. They are willing to compromise their integrity for money or for food or for pleasure or to save their own lives. We all are. It might not even be their integrity that's at risk, but the integrity of society, for which they have no regard.'

'Including you?'

Now he turned away again, back to the street, to the distance. 'Especially me, dear boy. I will do and have done almost anything for money.'

'You've killed a child?'

'I have.'

'I'm not sure that I want to paint you.'

'Why? Because you suddenly find me distasteful?'

'I would find myself distasteful.'

'You would learn to live with it. We all do. Did you believe as a child that you would become a drunk in an attic? If you had known, would you have killed yourself? Of course not. We learn to live with our failings, Jumeau.'

He moved out of the sunlight and back into the cooler shadows. His feet bordered a rhombus of dust-blighted light upon the aged, naked floorboards.

'Tell me about your commission. Hold nothing back. Don't be coy.'

'It's for a small oil company. At the moment they are only national, but they hope to be worldwide in a couple of years.'

'And what do they want you to say in this commission? Let's call it what it is, shall we? What do they want you to say in this advertisement?'

Jumeau shrugged. 'The same as everyone else. How great they are.'

'Some kiddies in the back of a car having fun and games, while mom fixes her makeup in the vanity mirror, while pop pumps gas into his ten miles per gallon stallion?'

Jumeau crossed his arms. 'Something like that.'

'I'm surprised you would do that for so little.'

'First of all, you don't know what I'm being paid and secondly, I don't see why it should be such a surprise.'

'You don't? Really?'

'I don't. Really. Jeez!' Jumeau rubbed his eyes. He suddenly felt very tired. He was out of practice. 'It's way too early for this philosophical bullshit.'

'It's never too early for philosophical bullshit, Jumeau. To take your first point – if you were being paid more than ten thousand dollars, or even close to it, you would have thrown me out quite some time ago. The fact that we are negotiating,' he paused at the word, 'suggests that it is somewhat less. As to your second point...Does it not occur to you that by promoting these people you are contributing to the deaths of hundreds of thousands of people a year, around the world, many of them children?

'Well, I don't see how. I just do what I do and that's that.'

'You believe in the disconnection?'

'I choose not to believe in the connection. There is no benefit to the connection. I believe in the dismantling of my personal responsibility and the absolute severance of myself from others.'

'Oil runs our vehicles, Jumeau. Our vehicles dominate our towns. Our towns are shrouded in smog. People with chest and heart problems are more likely to die in heavy smog. People get run down by cars, cars that are run upon the oil you promote in order to stay in wine. Countries that produce oil have a stranglehold upon those countries which do not.

Wars are fought for oil, atrocities committed, lands laid waste, people starved.'

'How other people behave is not my responsibility.'

'You are a part of the chain.'

'I am a random event. A cluster of atoms. My intentions are not to cause war or to bring poverty or wealth or pain or health to others. I don't care about them. If I have any intentions at all, which I seriously doubt, they are to paint, to eat, to add beauty to the world, to lay naked upon the canvas and risk the laughter and condemnation of others so that I can somehow present the world through my eyes.'

'To what end?'

'Just to the end, that's all. Just to the end.'

'You're all the same. You claim nothing, but want it all. You claim silence, but long to be heard. You claim innocence but are as bathed in guilt as the drunken man behind the wheel of his car or the renegade general with a penchant for loud bangs. You practice self-exclusion in order to avoid rejection and at the same time long for inclusion.'

'Well, you make me wish I hadn't opened the damn door now! I don't think I want to paint your picture and I most certainly don't want your ten thousand dollars. I've done pretty well so far without it.'

'Are you sure?'

'As sure as I've been about anything in my entire life.'

Wint snorted dismissively. 'Well, that shouldn't fill you with confidence.'

He gathered up his hat and coat from the windowsill. A tremendous heat came off them as if he had just picked up living things. His green eyes pierced the veil and gouged the street again. He appeared to see beyond the facade, beyond the flesh and the metal and the bricks. It was impossible to know what he saw; only that he did see. He was like a cat that could see and hear things among the long grass and in the bushes that remained hidden to others.

Yet, despite him, Jumeau liked him. He did not want him to go, but neither did he want his perceptions or his truths. Yet he so enjoyed his perceptions and his truths, his badinage, his attack, attack, attack and his willingness to defend by further attack. Jumeau had shed his truths long ago upon the back of pain and disappointment and would no longer acknowledge the influence of the outside world.

'I shall go,' said Wint.

'Five hundred dollars,' said Jumeau with an urgent reluctance. 'They pay me five hundred dollars. Three commissions a year allows me to live at the height of poverty.' He felt shame as he spoke. He did not know why he felt shame, perhaps because of his submission and his admission. He had somehow sneaked into the confessional and shed tears for the priest.

Wint shrugged into his coat and placed his hat upon his naked head. It fell into place with practiced ease. He eased his gloves on, finger by finger.

'Then you will accept my ten thousand?'

Jumeau wasn't sure that accepting his offer was any less compromising than accepting work from the oil company, but he knew less about the man than the company so, by that rather feeble reasoning, said yes. Oh, of course, he nearly forgot. He needed the money. Laziness was an expensive virtue. He could be lazy to his heart's content with ten thousand dollars. Yes, he *was* a shameful whore, but at least he felt guilt for the calluses on his back. At least he felt the pain of this man's penetration.

'I shall come back on the morning of the fourth day,' said Wint with absolute certainty. 'Be ready. Have your paints prepared and your brushes trimmed. You will earn your money, sir. I shall see to that.'

4

When Wint left, his scent of citrus and cloves remained. Without him in the room, that underlying sweetness that Jumeau had noticed became more obvious, more cloying with the underlying hint of the dentist's chair.

He poured himself some more wine and went to the windowsill again. The sill itself was now almost too hot to touch and there was no breeze save the constant warm breath of the living city as its sighs and exhalations lapped and eddied up and along the overheated concrete. He watched the people some more, partly in the hope that he would see the blue-eyed girl again, in her summer frock with her ballerina's walk. He didn't see her, but he saw plenty of other pretty women who, with the sun, had discarded their drab cocoons and become butterflies. They did not walk, they flitted madly, between cars, from shop front to shop front, into office blocks and from person to person. As they went they sipped the nectar of experience and seemed to get a sugar buzz from each new one, so that they could flit further and taste more and so justify the time spent in the dark. Jumeau envied them their freedom. He admired their bravura, to go out into the world and take it on face to face without fear of falling or thought of failure and to embrace only the sweetness of it all.

If he could, he would. If he could descend those stairs and, instead of remaining in the shadows, step into the sunlight, put his arm around the thin, black-belted waist of a floral goddess and dance with her upon the golden sunlit sidewalk while the world passed by with nothing but smiles, he would. If he could, he would.

Curse them, all of them, he thought and lit another cigarette. He didn't appreciate it. It was too hot to smoke and yet the habit was harder to beat than the heat, so he smoked all the same. Everything, including those who teemed beneath him, was better from a distance. Once you got close, you were within reach of the body odour and the warts, the cancers and the venereal disease. Look, but don't touch. To touch was to risk infection. To become infected was to inflict a living death upon yourself. He longed to hold the floral goddess in his arms, to feel her warmth, to kiss her and feel the pillows of her lips against his. He longed to sit in silent admiration of her gemstone eyes that sat in those pure saucers of milk. He longed to feel the anticipation of copulation, the readiness, the willingness, the submission, the trust, but he did not want the act, for the act was the end. Once this was complete, once all had been shared, there was nothing but stasis and the inevitable slow decline into hate or, worse still, into indifference. To feel indifferent about anything in life was perhaps the worst sin of all and he could not bear to sin again. The punishment was too great.

A cab flared in anger. A thousand replies ricocheted, demented trumpets in a tuneless void that had been waiting patiently for the chance to blurt uselessly at the world. It was the music of the city, sidewalk jazz, skyscraper blues, the harmonious discord of the world colliding, the tectonic tunes of the engine age, tearing at the unsteady underpinnings of a fragile world. How it never fell apart astounded Jumeau, with its daily shuddering and night time rumblings. One day it would all collapse, of this he was in no doubt. Someone, somewhere, would say that enough was enough and cease to function and set off a chain reaction across the world. All would fall and mankind, those who survived, would become their true selves again, animals with an unreasoned passion to stay alive. There would be a financial and intellectual avalanche and, like a black hole, the human world would fold in upon itself and become a vacuum for reason, compassion and love, those things that we came so close to perfecting but kept at arm's length for fear of euthanising the animal within. Who was he kidding? It already was a vacuum. This thin veneer, this patina of civilisation, was wearing thinner day by day simply through overuse and soon there would be nothing left to show but the dry, bleached bones of decay.

He finished the tumbler of wine and went over to the canvas. He could delay it no more. The blankness of it still awed him, still excited and intimidated him and, buried inside him, was a small acorn of hope that, this time, it would be good, really good, beyond even his criticism, too good for the oilmen and the men in suits, the tie-wearers who were slowly choking themselves to death. There was the hope that it would be not simply a company cartoon, but a world-changing, world-shaping, piece of art that would affect human thoughts and actions for all the years to come. The acorn, of course, would fail to thrive and die upon the last stroke of the brush. The realisation of his inadequacies would be a blow and he would want to take the canvas in his hands and crush it, but he wouldn't, because it would give credence to his belief that he had wasted his time, that he had given away time that he would never see again.

How had Wint known of his idea? Was it all so predictable – the kids in the back, the mom at the mirror and dad at the pump? Was the blossomed forecourt, where nature went hand in hand with the maladministrations of man, so startlingly obvious? The sun would be out, shedding all in a golden light. The father in his crisp white shirt and homely rolled up sleeves, would bare his white teeth in a sugary smile and, instead of carefully watching the cents and dollars spin like a fruit machine at the pump, he would look adoringly with his sharp blue eyes upon his family while, behind him, the blue sky and distant mountains spoke of health and hope, of safety and of future, of a world unburdened and unharmed by the carcinogenic crap that he was vomiting into his shiny red, fin-tailed thoroughbred, which would, in turn, as it sped across the concrete pastures, fart lead-based toxins into the atmosphere and destroy the brains and lungs of those who played innocently in its invisible shroud.

He picked up a wide brush and ran its soft, yielding bristles through a clot of paint, then ran the brush across the canvas.

He worked and drank and smoked until the sun had passed and the day had commenced the pink- and orange blossom-tinged transition into a summer evening.

Satisfied as he ever would be with what he had done, he wiped off his brushes and stood back. What he had translated from his head to his fingers had come to life and now it had a pre-nuclear glow about it. The incomplete figures seemed to be no more than ghosts, a foreshadowing of their future, all frozen as if caught in the moment of detonation. The trees, as yet only implications of their final selves, looked like the demon heads of nuclear blasts. Thick tendrils, naked unformed branches, wormed towards the sky and obliterated the light. He could almost see them shimmer and glow, lit from the inside, although they were only shadow and light, an artistic tromp l'oeil, a trick, an illusion, an upside down and inside out of an alternate reality. My God, he thought, I am infected and hallucinating. That man, that stranger, brought his disease and contaminated me, left me with contaminated thoughts and broken perceptions. He said what he said and sowed the seed and I am left unable to see what I want to see, crippled, blinded, by his accusations of hypocrisy and guilt.

He closed his eyes and buried his face in his hands. Red paint bled from his fingers and made it look as if he was clawing at is face, trying to tear away the mask that he had worn all his life, to prise it from his skull and get at the truth beneath. He parted his fingers and peered through them at the canvas. His eyes danced wildly as he tried to make a different sense of his creation. He ran them up and down the canvas in strips and tried to give shape and perspective to each part. It didn't work. The children's eyes were Belsen hollow, their skin pale to the point of translucence, their unbroken smiles of joy no more than wide and silent screams at the horror of impending rebirth.

He turned away and went to the window, poured himself a tumbler of wine and downed half of it in a single, desperate gulp, then sat upon the windowsill and smoked. From the Dansette came the ghostly melancholia of Autumn, that stringed scream that to him always sounded like the sudden realisation of lost summer, lost youth and the inevitable decline into winter. He knew at that moment that Vivaldi knew his heart, that such a noise could only be born of secret torment and the beauty of pain.

Below, the streets hummed a different tune. They had the sassy cool of a confident night, when car horns did not rent the air but simply laid down an extra layer upon the soft jazz of clubs and bars, joined by the yelps of joy that emanated from the free mouths of workaday slaves. He envied them their freedom. He envied them their ability to sever work from play and throw themselves wholeheartedly into those precious, hard-earned hours. The world turned upside down; blacks became the masters and the whites their slaves as they fell under the spells of bebop and jazz. They drank at the black man's fountain and sat in the black man's seats. They sat at the black man's tables and watched them through holy eyes as the blues of the fields and soul became the hip-hop hymns of this god-forsaken pleasure church, where intolerance was watered down by greedy need and fell thrashing in compromise to the floor where they writhed in peace and understanding, laid for once upon common ground, upon the white sheets of purity instead of the white sheets of hate. Drink from my tap and I'll drink from yours. Drive the bus and take me where you please until dawn splits the sky with a purple, bloodied bruise as the sun hauls itself above the city and we part once again as enemies until the rise of Hecate and the rebirth of our moonstruck love.

Jumeau thought of eating but quickly dismissed the idea. He would stay here upon his perch and drink and smoke until he could drink and smoke no more, until his eyes stung and the neon lights began to melt into a midnight rainbow and all the sounds of the night became a lullaby.

He hated life and yet at this moment he wanted to hold onto it forever. In his solitude and his dreams he found peace. In his wine and his cigarettes he found his needs fulfilled. In his art, good or bad, he found justification.

There was a hole inside him that could not be filled. There were moments, like this, when he thought that perhaps he had overcome, but the emptiness soon returned. All was distraction, all was fleeting. He yearned for completion and yet knew that completion would destroy him, what he was, what he wanted to be, needed to be, was born to be – incomplete. All art was simply yearning, concrete for the hole in the soul, but there was never enough. It was too deep.

5

He saw her again, blonde hair and blue eyes. Although he wouldn't admit it to himself, he had been waiting, his salt and pepper hair swept back roughly by hurried hands after a cold wash in a calcified sink across the hallway. He had woken thinking of her, quite possibly had fallen asleep thinking of her; he couldn't remember. He had scolded himself for his juvenile stupidity and had forbidden himself from perching on the sill, next to the open sash, waiting for her to appear like a mirage through the heat haze that caused the road to shimmer like an oasis. He imagined her as he cleaned his teeth, materialising to the etheric sounds of the city.

Then there she was, his eidolon. He smiled and gave her the name. 'Good morning, Eidolon,' he said through tight teeth. He pulled his knees up and curled his arms around them, rested his chin between his knees. She danced still, carried on clouds, borne by an invisible hand. She was in the same dress and shoes and yet remained immaculate. Immaculate. The Immaculate Eidolon. Would it be possible to capture such a spirit? To keep it captive? For it would never stay of its own accord. Such a creature would not thrive in a cage.

She passed his window on the other side of the street, looked again in the same shop window as she had looked previously, her heels together, her toes pointed slightly outwards, then swivelled on the balls of her feet, tripped lightly towards the corner and disappeared.

The city filled her space. She became noise and colour, the scent of overheated concrete and exhaust fumes. His delight turned to mourning, his wonder to despair. If only he had the courage to pursue her, to set foot in her world and to not be afraid to embrace, to absorb, to be absorbed, to live.

He finished his breakfast wine and took a final, long, slow drag upon his breakfast cigarette. Nothing beat the first wine and the first cigarette of the day. The body awoke craving that which it had been denied by sleep, was at its peak of readiness. He understood the addict. He understood the need and the relief. He understood the need to live by spitting in the face of Death. He understood how to embrace death by risking his life. Each nightly fall into sleep was a victory against nature. He knew that he would never win, not in the end, but he wanted it to be on his terms, as far as he could.

The canvas beckoned, he went to it with a thrill in his belly and fear in his heart. He did not want to face the Armageddon he had left the previous day, but when he looked, it had gone. There was nothing but insubstantiality, the shapes of things to come; here a cheek, there a branch, there the spaghetti-thin scaffolding of a low-slung building against a blue summer sky. He breathed a sigh of relief.

6

The fourth day arrived. He watched its birth, from the slow glow upon the distant horizon and the fading of the stars, to the explosion across the rooftops, the walking of the shadows, as the sun ascended, declared its mastery, its ownership, and slid towards its zenith.

He hadn't slept, not really. Occasionally his head had lolled and he might have passed out, but the snap of his neck always jolted him back into consciousness. He had spent the night upon his perch and watched the metamorphosis of the city, the chameleon change as it adapted to the hour. It was a living breathing entity, the streets its veins and capillaries, as the small busy cells, the corpuscular bodies that throbbed and heaved along its length, lent it the oxygen it needed to sustain it. Its neon eyes lit the darkness. Its breath was the outpourings of gaseous exchange, the financial and spiritual by-product of the life brought to it by those same cells that traversed its hardened arteries. It was a symbiosis, the host and the parasite, each strangling the other at the same time as they fought to keep each other alive.

The Dansette had remained inert throughout the night. Jumeau had wanted nothing to interfere with the overture of the streets.

He had seen a man die.

At about one o'clock some black guys had swarmed from a club and spilled jerking and strutting onto the sidewalk. They had split like the Red Sea. One side flooded around a tall, skinny guy, the other side around what could only be described as more of a building than a man. Before Jumeau knew it, the Building was doubled over and reeling back into the tumult behind him, while Skinny, egged on by a sea of fanatics behind him, all froth and boiling waves, seething like a storm, danced on tippy-toes as he took a couple more stabs at the Building. It was like a dance – step, stab, retreat – step, stab, retreat – until Skinny was covered in writhing black arms that looked like snakes all over him and pulled him away. Skinny and his crowd ran away into the night, their light feet making no sound upon the sidewalk, as they dissolved into the darkness. The other group just stood and stared as the Building's blind eyes took one last look at the world and his lungs, starved of the life force they needed, breathed their last.

It seemed to take an age before Jumeau heard the sirens and it wasn't the police; it was the banshee wail of an ambulance. Knowing that the cops would not be too far behind the ambulance, the Building's boys, all save one, took off. They scattered like autumn leaves on an eddy of air. The one who stayed kneeled down next to the big man. He ran his hands over him as if he could raise him by touch. He cried. His shoulders shuddered and he lowered his head onto the Building's vast bloody chest while his hands wandered and hovered over the ruins of a man.

The ambulance came. Its sorrowful cry pierced the stunned streets and the heavy air. As it got closer - three blocks, two blocks, one block, a corner – a crowd gathered, all heads turned as one towards it, full of expectation and excitement and satisfaction at the upturn in the events of the night. There was nothing so thrilling as the drama of death and the debris it washed up. The white ghost of a vehicle turned into the street – it must have passed the Skinny gang somewhere along the line – with a dignified serenity. It took the corner at a maidenly pace and, as if on a Sunday drive, pulled up next to the eye of the storm. The two ambulance men got out. One went to the back of the vehicle and opened the door, while his work mate went to the scene. A couple of onlookers pulled the crying man away from the Building so that the ambulance man could see what he needed to see. The man, in short white jacket, white trousers and white shoes, assessed the scene in seconds, then went to the back of the vehicle with his colleague and together they unloaded a stretcher. They moved furiously and silently in their well-rehearsed tango. They wheeled the trolley to the scene and, with a struggle, loaded the fallen man onto it, then transferred him into the back of the ambulance. The doors closed with a dense finality and the ambulance spirited away into the same darkness that had swallowed the mourners and the murderers.

It had all been mad and silent excitement, a ripple on the continuum of night. Then the vacancy left by the Building was filled by passers-by. People walked through the same air that only moments before had held his departing soul. The seas had closed and swallowed up the evidence. It was a miracle indeed to make a single man so easily disappear.

Now, barely the memory survived.

Slowly the traffic changed from the skittish randomness of night into the juggernaut jigsaw of rush hour; the same cars containing the same people who went to the same place every day to carry out the same tasks. Chrome gleamed and threw back the sun. Dark glass winked at secrets held behind it, while on either side of the metallic river a fruit salad of people jammed the sidewalk, locked in an invisible embrace with those close by so that independent movement was impossible, nothing to do but go with the flow and drop out as they were magnetically drawn towards their final destination.

The knock at the door made him jump. He had waited all night to hear it, had been unable to sleep at the thought of it, and now that it came, it made him start, sent his heart racing, caused an excited panic to ripple coldly along the length of his body. He shivered involuntarily.

The knocks continued in the same heartbeat rhythm as days before. He wasted no time, strode across the room and tugged open the door. Part of him thought that there might be nobody there, that even the slightest hesitation might have driven Wint away and left him in an agony of regret at his indecision.

'Good morning, artist,' said Wint. He stepped in uninvited and stood in the centre of the room. Again, his smooth pale face showed nothing, but his nostrils flared almost imperceptibly at the bitter stench of stale tobacco, paint and body odour. On top of this lay the patina of smells from the street below; the mix of spent fuel, melted fat from the food vendors and electricity as it pulsed invisibly through the hot streets and the sidewalks and crawled up the insides of buildings. His eyes took in the tumbleweed bed, the age-stained coffee cup, the full ashtray and the half full tumbler of wine upon the windowsill.

He slipped off his gloves and dropped them into his hat, which he handed to Jumeau. It had become routine already. 'You don't eat?' he asked as he slipped off his coat.

'What?'

Wint's lips pursed impatiently at having to repeat himself. 'You don't *eat*? I see a filthy mug, a glass, but no plate, no knife, no fork. You don't *eat*?'

'No.'

'Then how do you sustain yourself?'

'I drink grapes.'

Wint's head bobbed in acknowledgement of the answer. His head appeared too big, too precarious, and Jumeau had to fight off the instinct to stretch out his hands to catch it in case it fell from his shoulders.

'Do you have a woman?'

'As in possess?' Jumeau shook his head. 'No, I possess no woman.'

'You must have at some time.'

'I don't see why I must have, but yes, I did, at some time, have a wife.'

'And?'

'She left when she found out that I loved another more than her.'

'Your art?'

'Christ, no! Myself.'

'So how do you meet your needs?'

'My needs?'

'Your *needs*.'

'Oh, I see.' Jumeau reached for the Chesterfields and lit one. 'If I wanted a woman, I would go to a whore. There is no guilt. There is no presence. There is no debt. Only the...*need* fulfilled.'

'And you have no company? No friends?'

'I despise the company of people unless it's on my terms and my terms are silence.' It was an obvious stab at the questioning. 'Is any of this relevant?'

'To what?'

'You're here to be painted, Mr Wint. My personal life has nothing to do with it.'

Wint tucked his hands into his pockets and took up his familiar lean. 'On the contrary. It has a tremendous amount to do with it. I want to know that we will remain undisturbed. I would find the continual interruptions of friends to be awkward and irritating. To know that you are not in the middle of an unhappy love affair or bound to the will of a wife or lover means that you have more freedom than you would otherwise have done. That you are not bound by the need for food means that you will not have regular breaks, if any, and that therefore the work will be completed more quickly and that it will have been more focused. All those things, those things that bind our lives and constrict us, confine us, rule us, these things pollute us. I do not want my image polluted by your experience. I want you to paint what you see, not what you imagine or what you interpret.' His bright green eyes burned into Jumeau. 'This is about *me.*' He looked around the room. 'Now, where would you like me?'

Jumeau found himself wanting on the one hand to throw Wint out and close the door on him forever and on the other to shake his hand and thank him for his honesty. What Wint wanted was, of course impossible. The damage was already done. Jumeau could not discard his skin. He could not unmake himself. It was simply not possible to unentwine himself from himself. Even photography, perhaps the most honest and direct of the arts, could not help but be influenced by the life debts of the photographer. Could Adams have done what he did to the countryside without interpreting in some way what he saw? To him a mountain was a monument. To Cartier-Bresson or Capa, war had a sad beauty and that was an entirely personal interpretation. How could this man expect him to paint him and remain impartial?

'I have two chairs,' said Jumeau. He indicated a threadbare armchair and the wooden chair that had been butt-buffed to a perfect shine.

'I have no preference,' said Wint as he examined the two from where he stood. 'Perhaps the wooden chair would be the less confining, the less intrusive of the two.'

Jumeau stood next to his perch at the window. 'How about here? The light from the window could illuminate you. The window would make an impressive backdrop. What do you say?'

Wint shrugged. His heavy shoulders rolled as if two continents had collided beneath them.

Jumeau picked up the chair and placed it next to the window. He stood back and looked at the angle and the light, nudged it two inches to the right with his foot and inspected the scene again. Yes, it would be just fine. There would be light and there would be shadow; there would be texture and depth and there would be contrast. There were a hundred things to be considered, a hundred thousand possible interpretations. Oh, yes, he would interpret. If he wanted a picture of himself, an image, no more, then Wint could rumble off to the Happy Snapper on Third. There he would find his unemotional, unbiased, uninterpreted self. Here? Here he would find his soul *and* the soul of the man who painted him. They would be forever joined on the rough canvas. Only a fool would ever think that a painting was just about the subject. The subject was merely a conduit, a vessel, to get into the mind and soul of the artist and for the artist to offer the world his interpretation of it. It was all about the artist in the end, because that was why the artist existed, not the *man*, the *artist*, to place himself in the world, to add *his* colour, *his* light, to make *his* voice heard and to hell with the subject. If people found pleasure in the pots and the pans, in the vases, the fruit and the velvet, in the hay and the wain and the glowering sky, that was fine, but if you wanted to know the man who painted it, the *real* subject, then look at the light, the texture, the emphasis of the paint, the colours, the unreal grafted onto the real to form the new, the interpretation, and understand that what you see is not what is seen but what is perceived, like life itself.

'That will do,' he said, his open palm inviting his guest to be seated.

Realising that the hat and coat would now be *en scène*, he picked up the bundle and took it over to the bed. The hat he placed upon the pillow, as if there was some sort of protection offered in its mildly elevated state. The coat he folded neatly, aware of its value, following the natural folds. There was every chance that Wint would be watching and he was not in the mood for a lecture on the moral ambiguity of coat folding. He was still amazed at how Wint could wear such heavy clothes in such weather. Just handling it made Jumeau claustrophobic. He could feel the weight of it by thought alone.

Satisfied he turned around to Wint in full expectation of some sort of coat-based advice and was surprised to see that his client had removed his tie and had almost finished unbuttoning his pristine white shirt. Beneath the pristine white shirt was a pristine white undershirt. Wint removed his shirt and automatically handed it and the tie to Jumeau, then began to unbuckle his extremely soft leather belt. That done, he undid his pant buttons and allowed them to fall to the floor about his feet.

'What are you doing?' asked Jumeau.

'Removing my clothes.'

Jumeau danced nervously on the spot. 'What? Why? Why are you removing your clothes? Oh, Jeez.' He put a hand to his mouth while the other flapped uselessly at the air. 'Oh, Jeez. You're queer! Is that what this is about? All these days? All that preparation? All those questions? Is that it? Just some elaborate foreplay in the hope of bagging a penniless artist? Is that it? Are you queer?'

Wint paused. 'No. Yes. Sometimes. But not today.'

His blubbery arms reached around himself and tugged the undershirt over his belly and his breasts with an effort.

Jumeau gasped. He winced. He could not help it.

Wint stood naked before him, but it was not his nakedness that caused Jumeau to flinch. 'My God,' he said.

Wint's skin, almost Parian pale, was criss-crossed by innumerable scars. From his neck to his ankles, there was barely an inch of skin that was not raised by hypertrophic lesions that ran like worms across snow or was hacked and pitted as if a blunt toothed blade had been dragged repeatedly across his skin until it had been chewed to an unrecoverable pulp and left to heal without finesse or care. Among them were scaly scars that had only recently begun to heal, that had formed moist crusts or bled still from the unconscious attention of the man's manicured nails as he slept or as he was diverted from them for half a second, long enough for the subconscious irritation to set in and bring his fingers scuttling like crabs to pick at the carcass of a long dead fish. Jumeau looked again at the discarded undershirt and saw that it was speckled by small roses of blood.

'My God,' he repeated. As if he suddenly realised his behaviour, he pulled his eyes away from Wint's torn, puffy flesh and looked into his emerald eyes. Now they stood out, those eyes, like flowers among the destruction. 'I'm sorry,' he said. 'I'm sorry.'

Wint, so like a ghost in the shadows, took two steps forward until the light from the window exposed the full horror of his devastation.

'Paint me,' he said. 'Scars and all.'

7

Wint sat upon the wooden chair. His legs were crossed, his hands folded upon the tops of his thighs. He was close to amorphous, so pendulous was his body, so distorted by the effects of gravity, that his entire being seemed to flow towards the floor. The scars cast their own small shadows. Some glistened. Some swallowed in the shy light from the window and, against his pallor, lent his body a lunar cast.

Jumeau took this all in with the trepidation and horror of one who walked through the remnants of a battlefield. Even if you hadn't been a part of the fight, it was impossible to disassociate yourself from the scene. Limbs, hacked from their owners and strewn upon the bloody mud, were your limbs. The blind, half-closed eyes that gazed uselessly into the void, were your eyes. And it wasn't for them that you felt the fear and the pain and the remorse, but for yourself. It was impossible for those poor broken souls to be anything but you, for all they did was to remind you of your own vulnerability, your own tissue thin skin, your own ulcerated eyes, your own fractured and severed limbs, your own mortality.

Many years ago, Jumeau had been corralled into going to a funeral, for many reasons. He hated the hypocrisy, the show, the ritual and the reminder. People cried at funerals, not for the one they loved, but for themselves for what they had lost and for the loss yet to come. We might well miss the dead, but not for them, for us, for what they did for us, for the hole they filled in us. The narcissist rarely got over a death. People broke because they came face to face with their own mortality.

'Why do you weep?' he had asked a pancaked and plump middle-aged woman.

She had looked at him as if he had shit in her lavender-scented bath. 'What kind of question is that?' she had stuttered through broken breaths. She waved a frilled and expensive handkerchief towards the grave. 'For him. I'm crying for him. It is such a loss, such a great loss.'

'Not to him,' said Jumeau. 'He is dead.'

'To me!' said the woman as her fingers pecked at her chest like a dying chicken.

Jumeau nodded, his lips pursed in thought. 'So you weep for yourself. I see.'

She had slapped him across the face with speed, accuracy and power. He was surprised at the reaction. 'It is not my fault,' he said as he ran a hand across his cheek. 'It is not my fault that you are mortal.'

She had been the dead man's wife. He had not known that. He had not really known the man. He had been bullied into attendance because he was a senior colleague and his attendance was considered 'good for the department'.

The only other funeral he had attended, excluding one for his goldfish at the age of six which he remembered vividly because it had been such a cold day and the ground so hard, had been that of his mother. He had not cried, even though he had loved her and he missed her, for he was already aware of his own mortality and hers and therefore, as he saw it, had no reason for tears. He had no sad memories of her, only happy or indifferent ones, so he did not cry. Her passing held no terror. People, family and friends had gazed upon him with their wet eyes and silently condemned him for his lack of emotion. They were wrong. He was full of emotion, just not theirs. He never saw them again, any of them, not out of spite, but because he simply had no need. Their only connection had been the thin thread of his mother and, now that she was gone, the thread was severed. He had no need of them. He had no need of them.

He had not known his father. He knew that he had been French Canadian (his mother had been French and moved to Canada with her mother when she was six) and he knew that he had died somewhere at some time of something, but then that was his curiosity fulfilled. He had never understood those who believed, deeply, that he should be traumatised by a lack of parental steerage, that he should become effeminate because his life was somehow unbalanced, full of feminine bias, lacked the stench of testosterone or that vital ingredient that went into baking the perfect human cookie. His reasoning, not even actually stretching to reason, his response, without thought, was that why should he miss something that he had never had? His mother provided him with what he required. She had been a strong and reliable woman who had the ability to appreciate what she had lost and move on. She never spoke of his father voluntarily, but when Jumeau asked her about him, merely in childish and idle curiosity, she had given him a glowing reference. So, Jumeau had been left with the impression of a good man who had made a good impression upon others, but was now dead.

'I have to sketch you first,' he said to Wint. 'I would not normally do so but feel that it would benefit me on this occasion.'

Wint showed no reaction. 'So long as it benefits me too.'

'I'm sure it will,' said Jumeau. 'It will add value to your purchase.'

'You would not normally sketch your subject?'

Jumeau shook his head as he rested a pad of paper upon his lap. 'No. I find it too confining. It takes away spontaneity, but in your case...'

'In my case?'

'So much money...'

'So many scars...'

'You said that I was to leave out my emotional interpretation. Removing the immediacy of my reaction will distance me from my emotions.'

'I see.'

'I will sketch you today, prepare my canvas this evening, then tomorrow we can start to immortalise you.'

'As you wish.'

Jumeau picked up a charcoal, but then put it and the pad down on the floor next to him and went to get himself some wine and a cigarette. 'Can I get you something?'

'No.'

'A cigarette? A drink?'

'No.'

Jumeau tapped at the packet of Chesterfields, pulled out a cigarette, smelled it because he loved the smell of still fresh, slightly moist and rich tobacco, and lit it. The sulphur from the match flared and sent out a plume of blue smoke. He could taste the sulphur on his tongue as he took a drag. He frowned at the taste but accepted it as part of the ritual.

He returned to his position, where he knew his easel would be, picked up his pad and stick of charcoal and set the charcoal to the paper.

'I'm sorry,' he said. 'For my reaction.'

'It's fine,' said Wint flatly.

'All the same, it was rude.'

'An honest reaction is rarely rude if it is properly interpreted. Rudeness would have been to ignore it, to pretend it did not exist and exclude it altogether. To dismiss such a substantial part of me would indeed have been rude.'

Jumeau nodded appreciatively. Even as he spoke another welt appeared upon Wint's left shoulder. Wint winced and tried to pull away from the pain, but it simply followed him, stuck there like a leech.

Jumeau, reluctant to stare and yet unable to tear his eyes away, watched in fascination as, from nowhere, the vermicile bleb rose from Wint's pale flesh. It bloated like a swollen lip. As it grew in both length and height, Wint screwed up his eyes, his upper arm and shoulder tight, his neck muscles rigid, all to resist the pain from which they could not retreat. The skin around the lesion grew taut until eventually, to Wint's relief, it burst and a tear of blood rolled down his pale, corpulent arm.

Jumeau put down his pad and charcoal, went into his work area and returned with an aged, paint-stained cloth. He pressed the filthy rag against the wound. Wint did not attempt to stop him, but leaned into the cloth as if the gesture brought some relief.

'Thank you,' he said.

Jumeau continued to press. He could feel the warmth of Wint's blood as it seeped through the cloth. With the bursting of the dam however seemed to come some relief. Wint slowly began to relax. He breathed out through his nose as if he had been holding his breath and was afraid to breathe again in case it brought back the pain.

Jumeau lifted the cloth. The bleeding had slowed. A tattoo of blood stained Wint's pallid skin as if someone had swatted a giant, blood-sated mosquito against his fleshy arm.

'I'll get some water to clean it, said Jumeau.

'You don't have to,' said Wint breathlessly. 'Really. No trouble. No trouble.'

'It's not trouble, Mr Wint.'

Jumeau crumpled the damp cloth into his fist as if the act of hiding it could negate what had passed, could deny the loss of blood.

He left the room and went across the landing to the bathroom. It still sat in shade as the sun had not yet traversed the house. He disliked this room with its constantly dripping bath tap, its mildew and its grimy, encrusted porcelain. It wasn't because of its filth, but because it reminded him of his poverty, of the down and out that he really was. When he bathed in the stained tub, he seemed always to come out filthier than when he had gone in. That wasn't true, of course, but that was how he felt.

He ran the cloth under a tap. The water turned red as it passed through and dribbled into the sink, down the dark plughole. Pink rose petals of water clung to the sides of the sink and left behind them as they fell a ruby sediment.

How odd this man Wint was. He denied himself wine, fluid of any sort, and cigarettes, and would not accept food, yet had been prepared to bleed naked before a stranger. Not only that, but he had tried to hide his pain as his skin had erupted, then accepted the ministrations of that stranger, a stranger from whom he would accept no sustenance. How wonderfully complicated he was.

Jumeau looked in the tarnished mirror that hung like an empty, green-edged Polaroid against the filthy wall. He was surprised to find himself smiling. He didn't realise that he did that any more. The very thought straightened his lips. He wrung the rag thoroughly, dampened it, then returned to his room.

Wint had not moved. It was as if, in Jumeau's absence, he had switched himself off. Upon seeing the artist, he seemed to slip from his fugue state and suddenly notice that the world still turned.

Jumeau pressed the cloth against Wint's shoulder and gently wiped at the blood. It had dried quickly and stained. As he ran the damp cloth across it, it smeared like paint flowing from the thick bristles of a brush. He felt a little hypnotised by the trail, by the striations left in the cloth's wake, by the way the blood went from dark to light like watercolour paint upon a particularly perfect paper.

'There,' said Jumeau. 'I think we have it.'

Wint did not, as most people would, look at the wound. 'Thank you,' he said. 'I'm grateful.'

Jumeau tossed the cloth away and watched it fall at the foot of the easel. 'Sure. If it's okay with you, I'll carry on.'

'Of course,' said Wint. 'Carry on.'

Jumeau lit recovered his pad and charcoal from the floor. He was hot. He could feel sweat as it crawled from beneath his hair and continued down his forehead. Part of him wanted to check that that he had not developed a wound and that it was not blood that trickled down his face. He raised his hand as if checking proportions and surreptitiously ran his little finger through the moisture. It felt thick and slick and resistant to the pressure and he felt a panic begin to rise in him. He brought the finger down quickly and as it passed his eye he glanced at it. It shone with sweat, no more.

'It's not contagious,' said Wint suddenly.

Jumeau wiped his finger against his trouser leg. 'Of course.'

'In case you were wondering.'

'I wasn't.'

'Good. It's just that some people...'

'Yes?'

'Some people believe that these things can be caught through the pictures of magazines or the television screen or the miasma of the streets.' Wint's fat tongue squeezed from between his ripe lips and licked them. 'It is an affliction. It is not a disease. I am afflicted. I am not diseased.'

Jumeau felt uneasy. It was bizarre enough to have a large naked man in his room, even though he was an artist, but to discuss personal issues was not something that he liked to do. Of course, he was as curious as a cat, but he would not pursue that curiosity because he did not want to know, not really. With knowledge came awareness and with awareness came obligation and with that came care. He did not want to care. He had done caring. He had served that sentence long ago. He would not commit that crime again.

'Okay,' he said, in the hope that it would be non-committal enough to kill the conversation. He returned to the sketch. 'Would you like some music? I have a selection.'

'No.'

Jumeau turned his attention to the window and beyond. He tried to make his own music from the rhythm of the streets. He tried to pick out each sound and each note; the syncopated hiss of bus doors and airbrakes, the ubiquitous horns, the shouts and screams and laughs of the shuffling choir, the swell and fall of engines big and small and underpinning it all, the thrumming, rumbling bass of the city itself. It was all there. The self-perpetuating soundtrack of life. Even after the people and the traffic had finally submitted to the inevitable fall of humanity, there would always be a tune to be played, whether it was the sound of nature growing or the solar winds of final destruction; there would always be a tune, always a fiddle to be played.

And while Jumeau thought, Wint sat unblinkingly upon the chair, half in sun, half in light grey shadow, his shoulder glinting as fibrinogen knitted itself like armour across the wound. What man would submit himself to this? What man would allow his nakedness to show and all in the name of vanity? *Paint me, scars and all,* he had demanded. Was he brave and selfless? Or was he so vain that he wanted even his wounds to be seen by the world? Did he feel no shame for his deformations? Wasn't he afraid of being mocked and excluded? In his suit, he was no more than an over-fed, baby-faced man, protected by his bespoke armour, but if he exposed himself naked before the world...

Presumably, judging by the number and age of the scars that Jumeau had been able to see, this was a lifelong affliction. He had hidden behind a cloth shield all his life. Why would he choose now to suddenly expose himself to the savagery and intolerance of the human race? Even to show himself to Jumeau was to risk ridicule, to take for granted the integrity of the artist, to trust that, like a doctor or a lawyer, he would not break the confidentiality implicit in their contract. It was a lot to put on trust, especially as, in the end, it was Wint himself who was Judas at the table.

Like most creative types, Jumeau's felt himself susceptible to the easy judgements and oversensitive infatuation of one who peered too closely, in god-like fashion, upon the world. It was in their nature to wear their heart upon their sleeves, the actors, the poets, the authors, the artists, the righteous recorders of order and chaos who revelled in the elevation and dismantling of gods and men. It was impossible for them not to share, to try to divine from the actions and responses of others their place in the world. Their very insecurities made them prone to betrayal, iconoclasts, slaves to pandemonium, for it was only they that mattered in this diverse quilt of a world, only their opinions, their thoughts, their interpretations. Anything else was just flotsam and jetsam, the fallout, the by-product, of broken communication and the rotten nature of mankind.

He continued to sketch until mid-afternoon. Wint remained motionless and silent upon his hard seat and must have been in some discomfort, despite his ample buttocks.

'That's it,' said Jumeau with satisfaction. It had been a long time since he had focused upon one thing for such a lengthy period. This was the problem with face to face clients. They brought obligations with them, especially those that declined wine and cigarettes. It forced you to work and he could tell by the end of the session that he had had neither enough wine nor enough nicotine. He had found, strangely for him, that he had been sensitive to the needs of another. He did not want to infect Wint's wounds with cigarette smoke and he did not want to cause him discomfort by asking him to sit for so long in a single posture while he worked. Yes, it had been the doing of Wint, had been *his* responsibility - he had been the one to decline the luxuries and breaks, not Jumeau - but all the same, Jumeau felt an obligation to the man and he thoroughly disliked the sensation.

Wint stood and stretched his sinews. His great body blocked the light from the window. Jumeau pitied anybody who happened to be looking out of their window across the road at this precise moment. They would have caught quite an eyeful.

The wound in Wint's shoulder was raw. It would heal, no doubt, as all the others had healed, but it was raised upon a red slug of inflammation that promised to be taut and painful for some days yet.

Wint picked up his clothes and dressed. He dressed as if unhurt. He never winced or shied away from the touch of the heavy and expensive materials and, when he had finished, no one would ever know of the wounds and scars that he carried. All they would see would be the striking green eyes, set in a pillow of untainted and unnatural flesh. Jumeau wondered how he could stand the weight of all the layers, especially in this heat. It was almost at the hottest part of the day, when the concrete had soaked up all the heat that the day had to throw at it and now began to send it back, to thicken the air, take the humidity up that one unbearable notch and suck out the oxygen so that each movement became an effort. Each step Wint took must have caused the material to rub against the unhealed lacerations. It must have been like swimming through the glutinous stinging tentacles of a thousand jellyfish.

He suddenly realised that he had left the sketch open to view. He grabbed it and turned it over so that Wint would not see.

'It's alright,' said Wint. 'I don't want to see it. Not yet. I understand how precious you artists can be about work in progress.'

Jumeau put the pad upon the easel against the empty canvas. Wint put on his heavy coat and put his hat perfectly upon his head, then slowly and precisely pulled his gloves on.

'I would like to take you to dinner tonight, if I may,' said Wint matter-of-factly. 'To thank you. For your kindness.'

'That's not necessary,' said Jumeau. 'It was a purely selfish act. You were delaying my work. It was quicker to help than to simply watch you bleed. Suppose you had passed out through pain or blood loss? Where would I have been then?'

'Never the less...'

'No,' said Jumeau quickly. 'I don't do outside. Not unless absolutely necessary.'

'A simple meal...'

Jumeau shook his head. 'There is no such thing as a simple meal when one man buys another man his dinner. I am quite happy to dine upon your thanks, Mr Wint.'

'Could you not break the rule, just this once?'

'No. I prefer not to. My days of collision and consequence are over.' Jumeau took a step towards the door in the hope that it would encourage Wint to leave. *You see,* he said to himself. *You have forced yourself into politeness. This morning you could have told him unequivocally to fuckoff. Now, you inch towards the door like an awkward socialite at the wrong ball.*

'Don't you miss it?' Wint went to the window and stared predatorily at the streets. 'Look at it. All life is down there, in that one square mile that is visible from this window. The good, the bad and the ugly.'

'I know,' said Jumeau. 'I see it every day. I need none of them.'

Wint pulled his eyes away and, to Jumeau's relief, headed for the door. 'Well, if you change your mind...'

'I won't.' Jumeau cursed the unwilling half-smile that had crossed his face in an effort to remain kind, to not offend.

'I shall ask you each day. I hope one day that you will have whatever it takes to say yes.' Wint closed a giant hand around the door knob. 'There comes a time when we all have to move on, you know.'

Before Jumeau could reply, Wint opened the door and left, closing the door silently behind him.

Move on? Move on? From what? What did that mean? As if he had somewhere else to go! As if the world waited with bated breath while he decided to pierce his dull cocoon and emerge better for his hibernation, for the metamorphosis. Into what? He had changed all he would ever change and gone as far as he could. Life itself had been that sleep, that cocoon, that path to transformation. Now he was simply a residue of what was. It was his choice. He had moved on, damn the man! He had moved on and shed those cumbersome attachments that cause us to linger in a state of stasis, those emotional weights, those paraphysical delusions that threatened to cripple you and hinder every step towards completion. They were gone, all gone, and he was whole again, as whole as the day he was born but, as they said in the advertisements, with added extras; wisdom and depth and experience and learning and the knowing, the *knowing*, of it all. That was why he didn't do outside. The knowing of it all.

Jumeau put his ear to the door but could not hear the receding footsteps of the giant. What was he doing? Was he waiting outside the door in the hope that Jumeau would change his mind, like some spurned lover or creditor calling for his overdue share? Lunacy. He would challenge him, him and his moving on and his invitation to feed at the trough. He would whip open the door and tell the man to go, to come back tomorrow as agreed and not before.

He pulled the door open, ready to let loose upon Wint, but there was no one there. Only the shadows had moved as the sun had crossed the sky. It was as if he had stepped into a long-abandoned haunted house in which resided the residue of souls long gone, forever trapped within the stone and doomed to walk the same path for eternity.

Jumeau closed the door and leaned against it. He was full of regret, but he was also full of smug satisfaction with his ability to continue to turn his back upon the world. His regret would die, as all emotions died. He would smother it in the crib. It was an unwanted bastard, fathered in the heat of the moment, the product of easy virtue and naivety. These misshapen mishaps were born to die an early death for they could bring nothing to this world but heartache and pain and the disabilities that came with the burden of unneeded weight. Besides, what was there to regret? Nothing. If he wanted freedom, he merely had to step out of his door and step into the throng, but his exile was his island, his exile *was* his freedom. He was surrounded by the safe sea of cynicism, by the deep waters of pride and the constantly swirling eddies of self-preservation and fear. No man is an island? *He* was, because he chose to be. He had been a part of the continent and found the unwanted meanderings of others to be too much. They had to cross the borders, the boundaries, and invade his sanctity, so he had poured the waters of scorn and rejection around himself and created his island, this holy island, this monument to isolation.

He poured himself a tumbler of wine and downed it in one go. It flooded him. It drowned him. His short abstinence had paid dividends. He found comfort in its warm smother love. He felt its warmth as it fell into his stomach then filtered into his blood stream, into the smallest capillaries at the very tips of his fingers, then filter through the rest of his system until, finally, his brain told him that all was right with the world, that all thought had been crushed by the weight of the warmth, that there was now distance between him and his demons. He filled the glass again, drank half of it, lit a cigarette and went to the window. There was no sign that a man had died fifty feet away less than twenty-four hours ago. He wondered where the Building was now. Was he simply a piece of meat in a fridge at the morgue, on the verge of dissection by the coroner? He would be carved as skilfully as any other cattle and his cause of death written in medical scrawl upon a death certificate, the final reminder of his life and death upon this earth, his epitaph. Perhaps he was a ghost left to perpetually wander the sidewalk where he had died, to relive his death over and over again as the solid side of life trampled over his ethereal remnants, unaware of his presence, pre- and post-mortem. Or did he go to Heaven? Or Hell? Did being murdered automatically get you into Heaven, no matter how dreadful you might have been in life? Maybe Heaven and Hell did not exist. Maybe the idea of actions and consequences was simply a ruse, a way to get people to bend to the will of the wealthy and the powerful. Maybe we simply leapt into the empty vessel that was a newborn and started all over again. Or maybe we were just dead. Maybe the Building, that poor man, had had his chance, had done his time, and that was that. The world simply rubbed its hands clean of his dust and carried on. That was a terrifying thought. Jumeau knew that he would rather suffer the tortures and pains of Hell than nothing at all. At least in Hell you knew that you were in some way in existence, that what had come before had had an impact upon what was become. For there simply to be nothing...for there simply to be nothing...he shivered at the thought of it. Did we really do all that we did, suffer all that we suffered, to simply become nothing? If that was possible, to become something that was not. He was afraid of the darkness. What would happen if man suddenly found out that there was definitely no God, no after-life, no Heaven, no Hell, no purgatory, no redemption, no chance to start again? Would the law be enough? Those same laws were founded upon the superstition of belief in a god, in something better, greater, something paternal, maternal, all-knowing, in the idea that we could get our reward in the next life. The law would have to become Draconian, full of fearful oppression because once the mind was set free, the body would inevitably follow and the moral handcuffs of belief would slip away. Man would become beast. Everything that we held most dear would be destroyed if there was no God. In the end man would destroy himself, would become an unbound sociopath, because that was in man's nature. If it wasn't, we wouldn't need God or laws. The animal man would eat itself as soon as it scented its own blood.

He dragged on his cigarette and watched as the tide turned. Now, the people wanted out, they scrabbled to get their vehicles free of the city's gravity or walked tiredly but determinedly away from their cells, towards their one night of parole, a temporary pardon, before they rose again to push the rock to the top of the mountain and watch it tumble down again. Death was the only relief from such monotony. Maybe that was the reward. Release from the sentence.

He was hungry. He hadn't realised he was hungry until Wint had offered him the chance of food. When had he last eaten? Two days ago? Three? Four? That didn't matter. He was hungry, that was all he knew. He made up his mind to venture out to the diner downstairs and have something there. He would wait a while, until it calmed down out there, to try to catch the place in the quiet time, between the ghosts of day and the spectres of night, when the city fell into its own special twilight and it was safe for him to go to the lake and drink.

8

The girl behind the counter, all pony-tail and wide-eyed, lap-it-up innocence, bounced over to Jumeau.

'Stop bouncing,' said Jumeau.

'Good evening, Monsieur Jumeau,' she sang, white teeth, soft lips, hazelicious eyes. 'The usual?'

Jumeau sighed. That he should ever go to a place where he was offered *the usual* filled him with dread.

'Yes, Holly, the usual.'

'Coffee?'

'Is that a part of the usual?'

Holly giggled and smiled broadly. 'No.'

'Then, no, no coffee. Get me an empty glass would you? There's a girl.'

'Now, you now that you can't do that in here.'

'I'll wait 'til you turn your back.'

With feigned resignation she got him a glass from under the counter. 'I'll be back in a moment,' she said, picked up a cloth and went to wipe down a table.

Jumeau took the opportunity and filled the glass with wine from a flask concealed in his pants. He drank half and rested the remainder on the counter. The girl returned.

Jumeau looked at her briefly. She was pretty. Her ponytail pulled her hair back and exposed her neck and jawline and her perfectly proportioned ears. She was what people would call a doll. And those eyes, those hazelicious eyes, like the soft eyes of a rabbit. They could hold a man in their yielding grasp for eternity. She reminded him of Judy Garland, not quite the young Wizard of Oz one, too innocent and young, maybe the *For Me and My Girl* one. Still dimpled but with a twinkle in her eye.

Jumeau liked to pretend to be mad at her bounciness, but he loved it. She had *it*; joie de vivre, personality, enchantment, youth, a voice that was neither too high nor too low and was full of bubble gum and sex. Myohmyohmy...she was wife and lover, angel and whore, the perfect ice cream in the perfect bowl.

'It's on its way,' said Holly perkily.

'Okay,' said Jumeau. He picked up a newspaper that had been left and scanned the headlines. They were the same as ever, almost indistinguishable from any other headline on any other day. Sure, the words had changed, but everything revolved and eventually came back on itself in black and white.

'Did you hear about the murder last night?' asked Holly.

'As a matter of fact, I saw it.'

'You saw it? How?'

'From my window.' He gave the paper a shake and turned the page.

'Why, that's just awful! You must feel horrible about it.'

'Not really. It wasn't me that was killed.'

'I know, but...'

Jumeau took his eyes off the paper and glared at the girl. 'I saw him take his last breath. Saw the guy stab him. Saw him fall like a tree. Saw him die.'

'That's dreadful, Monsieur Jumeau. Just dreadful. Didn't it give you nightmares?'

Jumeau shook his head. 'I wasn't sleeping anyhow. Did they say what it was about?'

'Girls and money by all accounts.'

'Well, that's just lunacy. Girls and money indeed. There's nothing on this earth that's worth dying for, least of all girls and money. On the other hand, I am rapidly coming to the conclusion that there's not much worth living for either.'

Holly tutted. 'That's very sad. What about love?'

'What about it? Have you ever been in love? How old are you anyway?'

'Nineteen.' She hesitated and thought seriously before answering. Jumeau smiled inwardly at her thinking face. It was the face of an erotic Madonna. 'No, I don't think I ever have been in love, not truly. Have you?' She leaned an elbow on the counter and rested her chin in her palm. 'Have you ever been in love, Monsieur Jumeau?'

'I thought so once. I guess it was as close as you can get.'

'What happened?'

Despite himself, Jumeau found himself wanting to talk. He found it mildly unnerving. 'It turned out I didn't love her after all, only the idea of her. In the end she ran away with a car salesman from Brooklyn. I could do nothing but applaud her courage and sense of purpose. I would not wish myself upon any woman. If I could turn back time, I would go back to the day I met her and turn my back on her. That would be the least she deserved. That would save us both a lot of pain.'

'Oh, you can't have been that bad, surely.'

'No, I was just never that good. I was full of dreams and the more you dream, the more harm you do. Dreams strangle what's real. Take my word for it, miss, never try to live a dream. Make sure you always go into anything awake and with your eyes wide open.'

'That's terribly cynical. I wish I could find love. I wish I could get out of the city and find a farm and breed horses and wake up to crisp, sunny days...'

She stopped as someone behind her shouted. She turned, picked up a plate and put it down in front of Jumeau. 'The usual,' she said with a smile.

Jumeau took a large bite of his burger. For a man who was resolutely unbothered by food, he found it awfully good.

'Do you know what a genie is?' he asked.

'Isn't it some sort of fairy?'

'No, not quite. It comes from the Arabic word *jinn* and can mean either a good or a bad sprit. Can I tell you a story about a genie, if you can bear to listen to a man tell a tale between mouthfuls of burger and fries?'

'Sure.'

'Well, there was this fella went to one of those church sales. He wandered around for a while looking at all the junk people had brought in to sell, wondering what the hell people would want with second-hand watering cans and tatty pullovers, when his eye fell upon this old lamp for sale on a table. Now, it wasn't like one of those hurricane lamps or the kind of lamps you see in Humphrey Bogart movies, you know the kind?'

Holly nodded. 'Go on.'

'Centuries ago, in the time of Caesar and Cleopatra, they were like these small pots, tapered at each end, with a handle to hold it at one end and a thin, elegant spout at the other and between the spout and the handle was a reservoir of oil.'

'How do you know this kind of stuff?'

'I'm an artist. Artists know stuff.' Jumeau took a bite of burger. 'Anyway, what they did was put a wick into the spout, which soaked up the oil, lit it and gradually the wick burned away.' He started on the fries. 'Whatever, he took a shine to this lamp and asked the lady selling it how much she wanted for it. Two dollars, she said. Well, back then two dollars was worth all of two dollars, it was a good amount. He only had three dollars in the entire world, but he liked that lamp so much that he handed over his two bucks before he had too much time to think himself out of it.'

Jumeau picked up a French fry, ate it, then pushed the plate aside, drank some wine, wiped his mouth and lit himself a Chesterfield. The best Chesterfield in the world, in the history of the world, was the one smoked after a good meal. It was worth eating just for the cigarette that came after. Holly picked up his plate and put it through the hatch for washing.

'This old lamp,' he continued, 'was dusty as hell. It looked like all the previous centuries had found somewhere to rest in this one place, so he set it down on a table, got out a cloth and began to clean it. However, as he did so, smoke started billowing from it. His first thought was that somehow the friction of cleaning it after all this time had somehow ignited a residue of oil in the lamp and started a small fire within. Well, he put that lamp down and took three steps back, thinking that anything left in there that was combustible was so tiny that it would burn itself out in a second.'

The diner was quiet, so Holly came round the counter and sat upon a stool next to Jumeau. She put a cloth over her shoulder and rested her elbow upon the counter, then rested her head upon her hand like a kid lying on a pillow and listening to a bedtime tale. Her ponytail fell to the side. Jumeau thought how absolutely, ordinarily, beautiful she looked.

'Anyway, he was just getting ready to run for the door or a bucket of water, when through the smoke he could see a figure begin to appear. *Who,* he said, *the hell are you?*

The girl smiled at the way Jumeau told his tale.

'Well, the figure sort of drifted out of the smoke, all muscles, his thick arms crossed, turban on his head with a great big pink jewel in the middle of it, those baggy pants the Arabs wear on his legs and a beautiful purple silk waistcoat across his brown chest, and it turns out that he's a genie, with the top half of an Arab and those baggy pants sort of tailing off into a wisp of smoke, like a small tornado, which tethered him to the lamp, through the spout. You see?' Holly nodded enthusiastically. '*I,* said the genie in this deep, fruity Middle Eastern accent, *am the genie of the lamp and I grant you three wishes.* Well, the guy was naturally pretty surprised by all this but, convinced that he was neither sleeping nor mad, decided that he would, for the moment, go with it. *Okay,* he said. *I want a purse that never runs out of money. That is my first wish.* The genie says okay and waves his hands and wiggles his fingers and on the table in front of them appears this fat purse stuffed to the hilt with bank notes; tens, twenties, fifties, you name it. The man picked it up and weighed it in his hands, just to make sure it was real. Then he took a note out and, as if by magic, another one appeared in its place. He couldn't help himself, he started picking the money out of the purse and started to stuff it in his pockets. *No need,* said the genie. *It is yours, forever. Sew up your pockets, close your bank account, you will have no need of either ever again.* Well, all he can think about is what car he's going to buy, what neighbourhood he's going to live in, the sharp new suits and the boats and the women. Oh, the women.' Holly laughed at the way Jumeau's eyes widened with the excitement of the story. '*That's amazing!* he said to the genie. *I still have two more wishes?* The genie nodded and ran his fingers across his little triangle of beard. The man thought for a moment. He was aware that this was a once in a lifetime find, that he should be cautious and not waste his wishes. But, alas, he was also an impulsive fellow who, when given the opportunity, was not the type of man to squander such a chance. *I wish for my ideal woman,* he said. So, the genie, already knowing this man's mind, his likes and dislikes, out of the mists made his perfect woman appear.' He paused, tilted his head slightly and looked at Holly. 'She had black hair tied back in a ponytail and hazelicious eyes and kisslips that would have made an angel sell his soul.' Holly looked down and ran a hand self-consciously across her ponytail. 'She was everything that he wanted because the genie always knew exactly what was in a man's heart. Without hesitation, the woman came over to him, slid her arms around his neck and kissed him; it was the softest, most perfect kiss a man could ever wish for. *I love you,* she said in a voice that hit every note in every accent at just the right pitch. She was all that he had ever loved, all that he had ever imagined he could love and even the love that he didn't yet know. She was all. He turned to the genie, almost unable to tear his eyes away from this goddess, but drawn by greed to the bearer of these gifts. *I still have one more wish?* he asked. The genie nodded. *I wish,*' said the man, *to live forever.* Now, just for a fraction of a second, the genie hesitated, but he could see the impatience in the man's eyes and knew that, in his heart, this man was set upon an unchangeable course. The genie wiggled his fingers and waved his hands and closed his eyes and the mists swirled about them. *You have your wishes,* said the genie and all at once, in a funnel of smoke that was lit from within by orange fire and white lightening, disappeared back into the lamp.

Jumeau lit another cigarette and finished his wine. He was enjoying this. It had been so long since he had talked so much to such a woman; to anyone.

'What happened?' asked Holly.

Jumeau blew a long slow plume of blue smoke across the bar and watched it head like a willo-the-wisp towards the lights. 'Well, it was fine to start off with. He was ecstatically happy with his new wife and she was, of course, ecstatically happy with him. They both had a never-ending supply of money and everything they could ever need. Great cars, great house, they even bought a boat and hob-nobbed with boat society. He had a trophy wife, a trophy boat, a trophy car, a trophy house and a trophy life.'

'Ah,' said Holly. 'That's so sweet. A happy ending.'

Jumeau held up a finger. 'You would think so, but one day, that beautiful wish of a woman was out shopping and stepped out into the road right into the path of a big Mack truck.' He made a squishing sound and brought his hand down on the counter with a slap. Holly's eyes widened. 'Well, you can imagine, the poor guy was heartbroken, but it didn't take him long to realise that, with that never-emptying purse of money, she could be replaced by a new model every few years so, heartbroken as he was, he still had his money and his eternal life.'

'So, that's it?'

'No. All was fine, hunky-dory, A-Number-One for the guy. He was a pig in mud. Then, at the age of eighty-five, he got cancer of the pancreas. Well, he couldn't die and he could not be cured, so he spent eternity in unbelievable, unrelieved pain and in a perpetual state of dying, while those around him took money from his purse to pay for his care and to pay for their pleasures. There was a queue of people outside his door waiting to dip their fingers into his purse and there wasn't a thing he could do about it except lie there in pain and regret.'

Holly looked at him sadly. Jumeau thought he could actually see the beginnings of tears in her eyes. 'That's awful,' she croaked. 'What was the point of that?'

'The point is,' said Jumeau, 'that you should be careful what you wish for. It might come true.'

'So I shouldn't wish for horses and cold sunny mornings in Marlboro country because it might all go wrong? That stinks!'

'Like a low summer river,' agreed Jumeau. 'Like a low summer river.'

He felt a tad guilty for upsetting the girl. Just because he was miserable and bitter, that didn't mean that she had to be. 'Look, all I'm saying is that you should be aware, that's all. I once made the mistake of wishing for something myself and there was nothing I could do to unwish it.'

'What happened?' asked Holly.

Jumeau crushed out his cigarette and poured the last of his wine into the glass. 'It doesn't matter. Not now.'

'I'd like to hear it,' said Holly. 'I like to listen to you.' She smiled. 'Even if you do bring me down.'

Jumeau considered for a moment. He didn't like to talk about himself, didn't like to roll in the fetid stink of his own mistakes, but he was enjoying Holly's company and wasn't ready for it to end. He looked out the window. The tide was still on the turn. He still had time.

'A long time ago, when I was young and stupid, I got myself a job that I knew would not suit me. It would bore me to tears and frankly be too much like hard work. Anyway, I prayed, get me, *I* prayed, that I could somehow not have the job, even though my then wife and I desperately needed the money. I'm not even sure that I believed in prayer. I'm not sure that I believed in God. I always wanted to but it was more a god of convenience, a scapegoat god upon whom I could lay my sins and my troubles and shove out into the wilderness to leave me unburdened by conscience and responsibility, a sort of get-me-out-of-trouble-and-I'll-owe-you-one-god. He was there to see me through life and comfort me in death. My punishment to him, should he not hear my prayers, was to deny his existence, to obliterate him with a thought.'

Jumeau took a sip of wine. His eyes were distant, as if he was looking back into the past, at himself, as a father would look with love and despair upon an errant child.

'My prayers were answered, but not in the way that I had expected. The job offer was withdrawn because somebody with whom I had clashed years before found out about the job and wrote a nasty letter to my new employer.'

'What did it say?'

'They wouldn't tell me. They just said that I was no longer compatible with the post. Of course, I knew who had written the letter and I knew what it said because I was not free from sin and was perfectly aware of my past, but what was passed was past and there it should have stayed, buried.'

'Couldn't you have taken them to court or something?'

'With what? We could barely afford food. We found out very quickly that the law only works in favour of those who can afford it. If you have money, you have protection. Poverty excludes. Poverty oppresses. Poverty divides. It is a cancer that eats away at every part of the body of life until it smothers hope and you simply become one of the living dead. I don't have much time for God and I don't really believe in the power of prayer, but that day I had managed to rub the genie up the wrong way and he made sure my wish came true.'

'So now you live in an attic and paint and once in a while stick your head out of your hole in the wall in the hope of food?'

Jumeau frowned and shrugged philosophically. 'It's not so bad. I enjoy what I do. I am my own boss. I get to listen to the music I like and have no responsibility to anyone.'

The door to the diner opened and half a dozen kids came noisily in and parked themselves at a table. They were full of everything; youth, vitality, anger, happiness, hope, despair and all the other things that caused the see-saw of life to balance precariously upon the apex of the universe. Jumeau envied them all of it but, most of all, he envied them their time. They still had time, if they wanted, to pick up sticks and blast their way around the world, to record their songs and write their books, to make their Hamlet the benchmark for all the Hamlets yet to come, to find their niche in the world and be good at it so that when the time came for them to die, they could die a happy death.

Holly went and took their order. She was easy with them, bending with their breeze until finally they had made up their minds about how they were going to spend the next forty-five minutes of their lives. They didn't care what came after. They had the youthful confidence to believe that it would be fine, that they would never die a happy death because they would never die. Every day would be the now because tomorrow was simply of no consequence at all and the past had not yet placed in their way the bifurcations of the road ahead.

Holly put their order in and came back to Jumeau, behind the counter again now though. She leaned upon it, her chin at rest on the heels of her hands.

My, she was beautiful. Jumeau wanted to run away with her. He wanted to go and live in a meadow without snakes, in a wooden house that was warm in winter and cool in summer and where none of the frailties of humanity could be exposed because it would be impossible for them to exist. Yes, he wanted to love her, to see those hazelicious eyes stare moistly at the height of passion and feel her fingers in his hair as together they stared at the full yellow moon through the window of their home.

'You should go,' he said.

Holly frowned. 'Go? Go where?'

'Everywhere. You should take off your apron, throw it to the floor and just start walking. Start walking and don't ever stop. Walk around the world and, when you have done that, do it again, only along a different route. Experience everything; the sex, the drugs, the rock and roll, and do it all on your terms.'

Holly looked at him with a half-smile, convinced he was on the verge of insanity. 'I can't do that.'

'What not?'

'I have obligations. I have to come to work and help out at home. My mother relies on me, on my money. If I just walked away, well, I just don't know what would happen.'

'You would live.'

'I am living. Anyway, what about you, holed up in your apartment for days at a time?'

He looked at her with all the benevolence he could muster. It was too late for her. She was already trapped and did not realise it. Her happiness was dependent upon others and they were dependent upon her. Her fall and rise depended upon the fall and rise of others. They were knotweed, tied below the surface, bound, living the delusion of freedom in their rhizomatic daydreams. In a few years, she would be a mother, married to a man who saw the height of ambition as a job, a wage, a roof, a mortgage, two point four kids and a chance at the weekends to cut the grass and buff the car. Life for them would be just life. It would mean life, with no parole. It would be a series of thoughtless, invisible transitions through various stages until the final stage, like a wall, stopped them and ceased their beating hearts.

So how was he so different to them? He didn't want to think about that. All he knew was that he had had his chance and that he had failed, big time, that he was loathe to see the failure in others because it was an admission of recognition, but could not avoid it, perhaps because it gave him comfort, lessened his guilt, let him know that they were all in the same boat, destined for the falls.

'I had my chance,' he said and was surprised to hear himself say it aloud. 'I blew it. All I can do is find sanctuary. You know what I'm going to do now? I'm going to do what I do every day. I'm going to sit at my window and watch the day end and the night begin. Then I'm going to take a luke warm bath, prepare for tomorrow and then return to the windowsill and watch the world turn. What about you?'

Holly didn't even think about it. 'I don't get off 'til ten. I'll just go home, watch some TV, then go to bed.'

'What a waste!' scolded Jumeau good-naturedly. 'A beauty like you should be out there, grabbing life by the tail and swinging from it as it tries to escape your grip. You should control your life, not let your life control you.'

Holly's brow creased as if Jumeau had spoken a language she had never heard. 'I don't know what that means.'

Jumeau put a couple of dollars on the counter. 'That's okay. I'm not sure I do either.' He drained his wine and jumped off the stool. 'I'll see you.'

Holly smiled and opened her palm in a lazy wave. 'See you, Monsieur Jumeau. Enjoy your bath.'

'Of course,' he called back. 'It is the highlight of my day.'

9

The highlight of Jumeau's day turned out to be a tepid disappointment. There was no hot water, so he had to make do with a cold, quick dip. In the heat, it was undeniably refreshing, but Jumeau liked his bath hot so that he could open his pores and let the poisons flood out.

In retrospect, it would probably not have been the highlight of his day anyway. Wint, for all his oddities, was at the front of his mind. There was something very familiar about him, yet at the same time, he was another country. It was rare nowadays that anyone caused a conflict in Jumeau. He had practiced the art of disassociation and compartmentalisation all his life and had it honed to a fine point. He had always tended to make up his mind quickly about people and then either dismiss them from his life or keep them, but at a safe distance, on a silently negotiated contract that he could tear up at the first sign of trouble.

He disliked Wint immensely and also felt an affinity for him. He was rude and arrogant and comfortable in his money and yet those wounds, those scars, the way his pain erupted and the stoic way in which he bore that pain said that there was more to Wint than a suit and a healthy bank account. How many people had Jumeau dismissed over the

course of his life based on first impressions? Too
many to remember. It was perhaps his cardinal sin.
His wife had told him that he was an all-or-nothing
man. Hang 'em or hug 'em, there was no in between.
She was right. He had been an over-principled,
judgmental bastard, but he had learned that you
could have either your principals or your friends,
never both. Anyway, what were principles? What
were friends? Neither of them hung around long
once the going got tough; even wives bolted for the
door. He didn't blame the friends or the wives.
Friendship was a house built on straw anyway. It was
parasitic at worst, symbiotic at best, based on nothing
more than the mutual needs of the individuals. Like
the skin of a beautiful woman, friendship could not
stand up to close inspection; the flaws were too deep.
The face of even the most stunning woman still
crawled with demodex spiders and colonies of
microbes that feasted upon the debris in her pores.
Friendship was no different. It was mutually parasitic
and, if we put our friends under the microscope, we
would be disgusted by their habits and their desires,
most of which we practiced ourselves. In friendship,
once the cons outweighed the pros, that bond
dissolved like skin in acid. Murderers and perverts did
not have friends, not once people knew that they were
murderers and perverts. They reminded us too much
of ourselves. Even families disbanded in the light of

outrage and repulsion. Jumeau did not have a problem with this. It was human nature and we should always beware of human nature. What he despised though, was the pretence, the pretence that blood was thicker than water, that friendship lasted forever, that people would cling to you through hurricanes and tornadoes and hold your chin above water when the floods came, no matter the risk to themselves. No, that was bullshit. People ran for the hills and higher ground. It was amazing what heights low people could reach. There was always a certain pleasure to be gained from looking down upon the devastation.

He went to his easel and half carried it, half dragged it across the room, ready for the morning. Next he brought over a small table upon which lay his oils and his brushes and his palettes and his rags. He felt a tinge of excitement at the prospect. There was nothing as intimidating or as wonderful as a blank canvas. It contained all the potential for greatness, for immortality, for failure, for underachievement for creating myths from mortal men and for bringing those myths within the grasp of mortal man, for making the intangible tangible and for dragging the unconscious, the truth, the lies, into the light and screaming, 'This is the state of man'.

Of course, Jumeau had never achieved such heights. He had always set out with the intention of doing so but, in the end, he had merely reproduced. Each catchlight in the eye had been no more than a daub when he had intended it to be an illumination of the soul.

There was a soft knock at the door. Jumeau turned upon the balls of his feet, unsure if he had heard the sound, but it came again. His instinct, as ever, was to recoil. His reaction, as ever, was to resent, to begrudge. The soft knock repeated. It was full of uncertainty, of hesitation, maybe even of apology. It had none of the persistent determination of Wint. It was the timorous knock of a mouse, a mouse that had dared to venture out of its hole at the foot of the wall in the hope of cheese.

Jumeau bit the inside of his cheek and clenched his jaw. His eyes narrowed. He realised that, to an outsider, he would have looked like a nervous ape. My God, he thought, I have taken a step down the evolutionary ladder. I have become an animal in my isolation. A few days ago, when Wint had knocked, he had felt panic and fear as if he was the first man to ever see flame. He had suffered the cognitive blindness that accompanied them. Now, his limbic slumbers had been interrupted by the presence of a pale, scarred man. Was it possible that he was coming out of his hibernation into a new spring? He had spent a lot of time upon his perch in recent days, had even looked forward to it. Of course, he had been there a thousand times, but he had never found his Eidolon before, not before Wint had come along. And the murder. He had felt a shameful fascination in the toppling of the Building, had a sneaking admiration for the skinny killer, even envied his power, his ability to come to such an instant, memorable, world-changing decision. In the murder, the skinny killer had forever made his mark. He had taken a life and in doing so had stepped outside the bounds of normal men and become a god, because only the gods have the ability to create such havoc among the scared and the oppressed. The Building, that wonderful giant, who had survived for so long upon his size and his wits and then, suddenly one day, felt his immortality drain from him as blood seeped from his ruptured artery and dragged his life-force from him. He wanted to ask him how it had been to die, to know that he was at the zenith and the nadir of his life. Had he been afraid? Had he been curious? Had his death lived up to his expectations or had he believed in his own immortality until his last breath? Was he so deluded that he believed, like each one of us as we sleep-walked through our lives, that all would be well? Did the distant, sad wail of the ambulance give him hope, reinforce his delusion or did it make the transition that just bit more difficult? To be so near yet so far?

He opened the door six inches and peered into the darkness.

'Holly,' was all he could say. In the microsecond from brain to mouth, he flattened the girl's name, took all feeling, all surprise, delight, resentment, joy, fear and excitement from the intonation.

'Monsieur Jumeau,' said the girl with the hazelicious eyes. 'I'm sorry to disturb you, but...'

'Yes?' Jumeau heard his voice and wondered to whom it belonged. It was strangely distant.

'I was wondering if you might like to take me for a drink or go for a walk. It's a beautiful night. There's a grand, yellow moon...'

'I don't do outside,' said Jumeau.

Holly's face froze with a smile still upon it. It was not quite grotesque. 'Oh, well, I 'm sorry to have intruded.' She turned to go.

Jumeau opened the door some more. 'You could come in if you wish. I have wine, as you know, and we could look at the moon from my windowsill. It will still be as grand and as yellow.'

Holly bounced upon the balls of her feet, then made up her mind. 'What the hell! It's nineteen fifty-nine. If a girl can't have a glass of wine and stare at a grand yellow moon from the windowsill of a fella's apartment, then there's something wrong, I say.'

Jumeau opened the door fully and beckoned her in.

She had changed out of the diner uniform and put on a summer dress. It was bright yellow and patterned with flowers, which Jumeau thought were probably not based on any living plant. It was pretty anyway, feminine and, with her hair still in a ponytail, she had an abundance of youthful summer about her. As she walked past, he caught a scent of citrus mingled with the stink of fried food and cigarette smoke. He didn't mind. She was at the same time familiar and mysterious. He had never imagined her smell, had not really, until tonight, seen her as a woman, as a human being, merely an appendage of the establishment that he once in a while visited in order to stay alive. If it had turned out that she had breeze-block feet and cutlery fingers and that when the lights went out in the diner she simply remained motionless, with that smile upon her face and half a bounce in her legs, unblinking, switched off, in the darkness, it would not have surprised him. Until this moment she had only ever existed in context and it had not occurred to him that she might have a life outside the diner.

'I'll get you that wine,' he said. He went to his bedside table and from the cupboard beneath produced a wine glass. It was a beautiful glass, crystal cut and weighted through the stem so perfectly that it could have rocked between his fingers like a perpetual pendulum. From next to the glass he brought out a new bottle of wine and, with practiced ease, uncorked it.

'In the evenings,' he said, as he handed Holly the glass, 'I sit upon the sill and watch the world go by.' Holly sat down on the sill and turned to look out the window. 'It's like watching ghosts or a movie. It's so distant and unreal.' Jumeau poured himself a tumbler of wine and fought off the urge to devour it as a dying man tried to eat the air. He reminded himself that it would be fine, that there was more wine within reach. So long as the tap didn't run dry...

He sat down upon the sill in his usual position and encouraged Holly to do the same. Their legs slid next to each other with ease, hers next to the window, his upon the edge of the sill.

'It's hard sometimes not to believe,' he said, 'that it's not the whole world down there. I can't imagine that beyond the lights, over the skyline, around the corners, the world continues, that over the rooftops there is a horizon and beneath that horizon is China and Australia and England and small dots of islands in the pacific, where small children play naked upon the white sand while their fathers push small boats into a calm turquoise sea and paddle across the clear waters in search of a catch in their small nets. I will never know these people; they might as well not exist. For all I know they don't exist. They might just be rumour or figments of my imagination of part of a giant joke played by a malevolent god.'

He became conscious that he was talking too much. It had always been a problem of his. When he was nervous he had to fill the silence because if he didn't, the silence would crush him, but by filling the silence he found himself crushed by his own bleating crassness, his own stupidity, his inability to relate to people face to face. He had never like the interaction and, when he was young, had often found himself running out of words. People then took the opportunity to flee and he was invariably left in a vacuum of his own making where it was impossible for anything to thrive. That was probably why he had the need to fill the gaps, to distract himself from the discomfort. But, in his attempts to say something useful, interesting, he found himself flapping like a fish, thrashing about on deck, skimming from puddle to puddle, taking in enough oxygen to survive, knowing that he was doomed to never get back to the sea.

'The tide begins to turn at about five am, when the big fish return to the reef. The night-hunters scatter, back to their holes, leaving behind the bones of their prey.'

'It's rather beautiful,' said Holly without taking her eyes from the street. 'It's like a living painting. I could sit and watch this for hours.'

'I do,' said Jumeau. 'Only, lately...' He lit a cigarette and gave it to Holly, then lit one for himself. 'Why are you here, Holly?'

'I was curious. You were different tonight, so talkative. Normally, you come in, order, eat silently and leave. You seemed...' Holly's lips closed around the cigarette and drew upon it. Jumeau noticed how soft her lips were, how full and, with their shape enhanced by red lipstick, how they resembled a kissable heart. 'You seemed angry,' she said. 'Were you angry, Monsieur Jumeau?'

'Just Jumeau,' he corrected.

'No first name?' teased Holly.

'I lost it.'

'Lost it?'

'Yes. I put it in my pocket for safe keeping one day and it fell through a hole. I haven't seen it since.' He smiled at her.

'I see,' she said. 'Go on. Were you angry, Just Jumeau?'

'No, I wasn't angry. Lately, in the past few days, I seem to have been...' He hesitated. Such talk was self-indulgent.

'Yes?'

'It sounds crazy, but I seem to have been coming back to life. It's as if I have been in a coma for so long and have suddenly awoken. I can see it all, the colours, the people, hear the sounds, smell the smells, feel the weight of gravity and taste the oxygen in the air.'

'That doesn't sound crazy at all. Maybe you have just been alone for too long. Perhaps it's just your subconscious telling you to rejoin the human race.'

Jumeau laughed. 'Then my subconscious clearly doesn't know me at all. I have run my race and have no intention of doing so again. It's true, I have of late felt a sense of urgency, but why? I cannot say.'

'You said to me tonight that I should control my life, not let my life control me. What did you mean, Jumeau?'

Jumeau sighed. Had the moment come to regret his diner bullshit babble? Perhaps this was the start of mania, where restless jabber took over until he was discovered one day naked, directing traffic, his privates flapping like castanets as his body danced the dance of the lunatic upon the hot tarmac of the road until he was dragged away to a room to be force-fed lithium until there was nothing of him left but a silvery-white soft-metal shell.

He leaned his head against the window frame and looked at Holly. 'For the first time tonight I noticed how beautiful you are.' She smiled and looked away and down. 'I'm sorry; I don't mean to embarrass you. How many hundreds of hours have I sat at that counter in discontented silence and failed to notice your humanity and your beauty? I have spent so many years just waiting to die. I have allowed my life to rule me, to dictate the passage of time. It occurred to me that I have not been afraid of death, but afraid of life. I have allowed the past to dictate the present and, by doing so, I have annulled the future. I have allowed myself to drift in the hope of hitting the shallows and finding dry land, to become a prisoner to the current, when all I had to do was pick up the oar, turn the boat around and see the island just behind me.'

'So what has changed?'

'I don't know.' Jumeau frowned. 'A few days ago, this fellow came and asked me to paint him. He offered me a lot of money, too much to turn down. It is since then that things have changed.'

'Perhaps he gave you a sense of purpose, that's all.'

Jumeau nodded pensively. 'Maybe. Maybe that's it.'

'And if you combine it with seeing that poor man die. That's pretty powerful medicine.' She leaned forward and rested her chin upon her knees. 'Shall we have sex?'

Jumeau looked into Holly's wide and hazelicious eyes. They were full of eager sincerity. 'Yes,' he said. 'We shall.'

10

Holly lay stretched out upon the bed. Her head rested upon her arms. Light from the window played upon her pale skin. It was bright. The pale yellow moon, a giant surprised face playing Peeping Tom at the window, had risen above the tower blocks and skyscrapers and cast a golden sheen upon everything. Holly's skin was wet with perspiration. They had each succumbed to the will of the other with animal passion. They had felt their way in the half-light, explored each other with hunger and curiosity. When she climaxed, Holly wrapped her legs around Jumeau so that he became a prisoner between her thighs. He had suffered the exquisite, painful ejaculation of a man long denied. When she was sure he was empty, Holly released him. He fell away as she put a hand between her legs and felt his warmth. She brought a finger to her mouth and closed her lips around it. Her eyes closed as she savoured the taste of their passion.

Now, Jumeau ran a finger down her moist spine. She squirmed with pleasure. 'That's nice,' she sighed.

Jumeau slowly ran his finger down between her buttocks and then down between her legs. She opened them and revealed the wet folds of private flesh between them. He put two fingers inside her and slid them back and forth. Holly raised herself into her knees, her face against the bed. She swayed with the movement of Jumeau's hand. He raised himself behind her and continued to slide his fingers slowly in and out of her. He grew hard again, removed his fingers and entered her.

'Harder,' she said. 'Harder and faster.'

Jumeau thrust forward with all the power he could muster. He slammed into Holly as she leaned backwards into him, to ensure that she could get all of him inside her, to ensure that he hit her sweet spot with all his force.

Jumeau came again. He held himself inside her while her fingers slid between her legs and rubbed herself until she climaxed again. She shuddered and then turned around, took Jumeau's still hard penis in her mouth and sucked the last few drops from him. He held her head in his hands as the final unexpected pulses exploded from him.

They fell in unison upon the bed. Jumeau lit a cigarette for each of them. They said nothing, but allowed the sounds of the night to drift up to the window and paint pictures of its own upon their now wide open minds. The Dansette threw out a soft saxophone from a dark corner of the room which mingled with the car horns and engines and laughter and shouts from outside. It all came together as a seething, soothing cacophony, an unintentional joining of the ridiculous with the sublime to create a synaesthetic beauty that filled the colourless void with meaning and a reason to be. This was joy unbound, thought Jumeau, unbound by rules and regulations and hang-ups that had lived long and fed upon the insecurities of the past. It said that there was no future and that there was no past, but that was okay, because there was a now and the now was all.

Jumeau, his heart alive in his ears, turned and looked at Holly. She lay upon her back, her eyes fixed upon a distant place. She was a beautiful silhouette, from her fringe to her slightly upturned nose, her full lips and her slender neck. Her breasts stood firm and her abdomen flat, the steady thrum of her aorta the only clue that the silhouette was real. Across her body small stars of perspiration caught the light and caused her to shimmer.

'Why do you paint, Jumeau?' she asked suddenly and softly.

A rough laugh barked from Jumeau. 'I don't know. I always have, one way or another. I've tried to stop, but I can't.'

'Why would you try to stop?'

Jumeau ran a finger across Holly's breasts, followed the contour of her firm, moist body. His finger left a trail in its wake, as if a rocket had passed across the starry landscape and left behind it a shimmering mirror. He felt her nipples harden as he passed slowly over them and circled the areola. 'To be normal,' he said.

It was Holly's turn to laugh. 'To be normal? What's that?'

'That,' said Jumeau, 'is what people expect.'

'You mean your wife?'

Jumeau hesitated. He wasn't sure that he wanted to plough dead soil. He sighed. 'Yes, among others.'

He said the words quickly in the hope that they would simply pass unnoticed, uncaught, and fall dead upon a barren land but, once released, he knew that they would take on a life of their own, without him.

'What is normal, Jumeau? You tell me what is normal.'

Jumeau thought he could hear Holly's voice crack, as if the question stuck in her throat. He looked at her and saw her bring the cigarette to her lips. Its glow lit her soft skin and caught the moist depth of her eyes.

'Normal is working,' he said in a voice so quiet that he couldn't properly hear himself. 'Normal is a regular paycheck. Normal is barbecues on the patio in summer and eggnog around the fire at Christmas. Normal is commitment. Normal is the absorption of the self by the two to create a new One. Normal is...' He dragged on his cigarette and felt a bitterness rise. It tingled within him and sent a shiver through him as if he had bitten into a particularly tart piece of fruit. How long had he suppressed such thoughts? Had he learned over the years that if he didn't like something, then he had to bury it deep, forget it, ignore it, deny its existence. 'Normal is sacrificing yourself for others and others for yourself.'

'Normal is bullshit.'

Normal *is* bullshit, but it's a part of the contract and you should always read the fucking contract before you sign. I did not. It was nobody's fault but mine.'

Holly turned onto her side and propped herself up on her elbow. 'Fault? What do you mean fault?'

'There is always fault and if there is no fault, there is only submission. Consummation of the one by the other. I could not be normal. I could not do what others do. I could not fit in. I tried, I really did, but I could not do it. I could not commit to the playground politics in which people indulge in every day of their working lives. I could not allow my identity to be owned by another. It was all quicksand out there, ready to swallow you whole if you took even half a step in the wrong direction.' Jumeau stubbed out the cigarette in the ashtray that lay on his chest. Small sparks flew and died as they fought uselessly for oxygen. 'Anyway, she left. She ran away with the car salesman. Did I tell you he was a cripple? He had a withered leg from polio and walked with a stick. Can you believe that? A cripple? I said to her, what does he have that I do not? *He can't run away*, she said. I thought she was joking until I saw her face and then I knew she was speaking the truth. He was forced by nature into compliance, in the same way that I was forced by birth to be an outsider. I felt sorry for him. The poor bastard. Not because he was a cripple, but because he just didn't stand a chance.'

'So what did you do, Jumeau?'

'I cried, for days on end. Then, one day, I stopped crying because I realised that I was only crying for myself and that it was a waste of time. I resolved to do what I had to do and to hell with the world. I came here without a penny to my name and started to paint. And you know what?'

'Tell me.'

'It was a glorious freedom that I found. My God, I couldn't stop. I just painted and painted, got some work from local companies, then with larger companies, did some portraits, even had a couple of exhibitions...'

'That sounds wonderful.'

'You would think so.'

Holly picked up the ashtray and placed it on the bedside table. She put her hand upon his chest and dragged her nails gently down his abdomen. His skin quivered with delight. 'I think so,' she said. 'It sounds like a happy ending.'

'Actually, you're right. It could not have been more perfect. I had the isolation I so wanted, the independence, the freedom to do as I wished, when I wished. But you remember what I said about wishes?'

'That's crazy, Jumeau. Wishes aren't real. They're like ghosts and gods, just another thing to blame our broken dreams and insecurities upon.'

'That's true, absolutely but, if you wish for something hard enough it comes true because your subconscious gives it life. There is always something that you do or say, a way you behave, a place you go to, that forces fate's hand and brings your deepest desires to life. You remember that job I told you about when we were in the diner?' Holly nodded. 'I realised later that it was not someone else that caused me to lose that job, but myself. I knew what would happen. I knew they would find out and I knew what they would do. And they didn't let me down. Of course, I was outraged by their behaviour, an innocent man struck down by the poisoned arrow of vindictiveness, but that was not the truth. The truth is that I was relieved, even it meant losing my wife and my home and suffering the humiliation that all that entails, because I could avoid normality. Thank God for cripples, thank God for vindictive bastards, thank God for fucked up pasts and the inability of the human mind to release the sins of others. I had slipped the trap. Sure, I had to chew off my leg in the process, but it was worth the sacrifice. What was the loss of a limb compared to the loss of my freedom? What was a hobble compared to the inertia of incarceration? It was nothing. There are plenty of one-legged men out there who have done very well for themselves. The thing is, it's all bullshit, this life. Nothing matters and everything matters. All or nothing. Take your pick. I choose nothing because all is unattainable, because the closer you get, the more you want. All is never enough.'

He sat up and threw his legs over the side of the bed. The night was at its peak. The heat from the city sucked the oxygen from the air. The humidity lay like treacle and made each movement thick and heavy. He went to the window and sat upon the sill, aware and uncaring of his nakedness. He poured some wine and lit a cigarette. Holly slipped from the bed and joined him. For all the absurdity of the naked human form, she still aroused him. She sat with her knees up and he could see the delicate moist folds between her legs. It had always struck him as strange that such a small area of skin could cause such untold misery and be the holder of such power. How influential the pull of the vagina was to a man. To fall from one and then expend so much time and effort trying to get back into any other. He had never known any woman to feel the same way about a penis. Perhaps that was why, unlike men, women understood the power of their sex. Women wanted power; men simply yearned for the womb.

He looked out of the window and saw two groups of black men spill from the club across the street. They were neon lit and moved like rainbows. A large man, as big as a building, grabbed a skinny man and pulled him towards him. They embraced and laughed deeply and loudly and sounded like thunder against the tinny sounds of the street. Jumeau stared at them. They seemed familiar, the big man as big and tall and broad as an outhouse, the skinny guy all bone and white teeth. The two groups mingled, arms across shoulders and around each other's waists as they strolled off into the night, all rolling hips and balls of the feet, and disappeared among the shadows and lights of a city night.

'Did you see that?' asked Jumeau.

'Those men outside the club? Sure. They were having a whale of a time, weren't they?'

Jumeau's face creased in uncertainty. Had he not seen all this before? Had it not ended so much more differently? Or was that just his imagination? It wouldn't be unreasonable for two groups of men to spill out onto the side walk on different nights and for the outcome to be different. Yet he could have sworn that they were the same people, the big guy and the skinny guy, the two groups all skitting on their toes on the sidewalk, halfway between a walk and a bounce, ready to run, ready to dance. Maybe it was just his memory blending the past with the present to come up with an amalgam, an easy-fit picture. Maybe nobody ever died on that sidewalk. Perhaps it was simply a dream, his imagination.

'I should go soon,' said Holly. 'I should be home when mother wakes up or she will worry.'

'Okay,' said Jumeau. 'Thanks.'

'For what?'

'For you. I know it can never happen again...'

'It can't.'

'And that's not our fault.'

'No,' said Holly. 'Not our fault.'

In the distance, over the skyscrapers and rooftops, behind tufts of candy floss cloud, the sky was turning pink as the new day bullied aside the darkness. The world paused, caught between tides.

Holly dressed and brushed her hair. Jumeau wanted to beg her to stay, for them to spend eternity in this night, naked and honest, upon his perch, and watch the world pass by, but he knew he could not. From the second he had opened the door he had known that this moment would come, that he would love her and that she would love him and that it would come to an end, but the moment, the now, was here and, for good or bad, the now was all.

II

Jumeau awoke on the windowsill, still naked. It was the sun, as it lay like hot gilt upon his face, that forced him into consciousness as, even in sleep, he tried to pull away from the heat magnified by the glass.

He opened his eyes and blinked gratefully at the life-giving day. He awoke with a smile, unsure if it was the residue of some pleasant, unmemorable dream or if the smile had simply not left his face after Holly had closed the door gently behind her. Whatever the reason, he did not recall ever waking up with a smile upon his face, even as a child. He did not feel tired either, did not feel that lag as if he had skipped across time zones and left something of himself three hours behind. He felt alert and ready to go, even to face the strange creature that was Wint.

In the street, traffic flooded into the city, a canvas of colour as the cars rolled bumper to bumper and, at either side of them, the gaily coloured office girls swarmed past their dull grey male counterparts. Jumeau smiled at the human reef. It was all so ritualistic, so bound by basic need and social design, yet it was beautiful and each fish shed its own colour upon its world and had its own part to play in the busy, bustling life of the reef.

Then he saw the girl, but she was no longer the same. Her wonderful golden blonde hair fell lifelessly, limply across her face, dark in its greasy rejection of the light. Her white dress was torn and stained and the prints of the flowers had run, bled into the material as if they had died and begun to decay. But, above all, it was her walk that had changed. The light, gay, ballerina footsteps had gone. She now lumbered, her right foot trailing behind her like an errant mongrel, her left foot heavy as if it had gone to sleep and never really woken up. She stumbled like a palsied blunder of birth. A string of saliva fell from her lower lip and swung willy-nilly like a wet web with each clumsy step. Yesterday, he would have given a limb to kiss those lips and thought it cheap; now he was repulsed by their dysmorphic, pulpous state. People didn't notice her as they passed by. She looked mugged, beaten, and yet she was all but invisible to those who flurried around her. She passed beneath Jumeau's window across the other side of the street, as usual. She hauled herself like a tonne-weight of coal. It was painful to watch, but Jumeau was unable to pull his eyes from her.

Suddenly she looked up at the window and held Jumeau's eye. She had become a terrifying prospect. Her eyes were sunken within a dark grey bandit-mask, and there was no life in them anymore. Her soft skin had become cracked leather as if she had been left out in all weathers, dried by the sun, swollen by the rain, excoriated by the winds. Her cheeks were hollow, her face skeletal, her nose waxen and pinched, her mouth turned down sharply at the corners and too big for her face, as if she had false teeth within that simply did not fit. Her proud shoulders, once straight and muscular, were now rounded and hung as if gravity had taken it upon itself to pull her bit by bit towards the ground. She held Jumeau's gaze for what seemed like a lifetime. There was no emotion in her face, just flat resignation. She turned away and disappeared around the corner. He was relieved. Unlike recent days, he had not today waited for her appearance, it had merely coincided with his waking. Had she always been like this and he had simply chosen to ignore it? Was that possible, to create such perfection from such a monstrosity just through imagination, through need, through pity or for whatever reason his mind had twisted the truth? No. It was not possible. Something must have happened overnight for her to appear in such a dishevelled state. She must have become ill, yet forced herself out of the house to carry on her life as she knew it. There was no other explanation.

What had he called her? Eidolon. His Eidolon. His broken Eidolon. The lustre lost from her blue diamond eyes.

He lit a cigarette. It tasted of nothing. The usual bite at the back of his throat and the slight nausea that always came with the first cigarette of the day, were not there. Not enough sleep, that was the problem. Everything was upside down and inside out. He felt so awake because he was exhausted, because of the joy he had felt in Holly's presence. He had woken up high and now he was coming down, the natural opiates in his system dissolving to leave him coming down with nowhere to stop.

There was a familiar knock at the door.

Without hesitation he jumped from the sill and went to the door. He opened it to see Wint with his hand raised expectantly.

'You are naked, sir,' said Wint.

'Now you know how it feels,' said Jumeau.

He walked away from the door and allowed Wint to follow him in. This Wint did and closed the door behind him. Jumeau noticed that Wint was not wearing hat, coat or gloves. The effect was remarkable. It was as if somebody else had entered the room.

'No gloves? No hat? No coat? Has it become too hot even for you, Mr Wint?'

Wint began to undress. As he did so, Jumeau put on some clothes.

'It is close,' said Wint. 'I put them on and felt encumbered, so took them off again. I think it unlikely to rain for some time yet and I don't see the temperature falling below Hell for a while.'

Jumeau, with only a T-shirt and a pair of blue jeans to slip on, was dressed in a trice, so put the chair in position for Wint and brought his easel and trappings across. Wint took his place upon the chair as if he had never left. As Jumeau glanced at him, he noted to his astonishment that, not only had the previous day's wound healed and left only a slightly raised area, but that even some of the fresher wounds had gone, some of them leaving no trace of their existence. He looked at the sketch he had done the previous day as a comparison and found that he was right. He had been faithful in his reproduction of the wounds and scars, every serpentine slither across the pale skin and every raised and knotted scar, to the point of describing their shape, dimensions and precise location.

'Mr Wint,' he said. 'Your skin...'

'I know,' said Wint. 'I went to bed looking like I'd rolled through a bramble bush and awoke well, like this.'

'But how?'

'I have no idea. The sun through the window perhaps. They say it heals.'

Jumeau looked again at the sketch. 'It's remarkable. The scars have stayed, but the fresher wounds seem to have gone altogether.' He scratched his head through a mop of untidy hair. 'What should I do? Should I paint the you of yesterday or the you of today?'

The corners of Wint's mouth turned down in what, for him, was a mighty flood of emotion. 'Well, that's a quandary. It hadn't occurred to me.' He rolled his fingers over his large thigh. It sent a small ripple through his flesh that reminded Jumeau of the sea. 'Could you possibly leave the scars until last?'

'Of course. Do you anticipate further recovery?'

Wint shook his head unknowingly. 'I didn't anticipate this, Jumeau, so I am not so far-sighted as all that. It just seems to be the wisest thing to do, under the circumstances.'

'The circumstances?'

Wint sighed deeply, impatiently, as if there was simply too much to consider. There was suddenly a distance to him as he looked beyond Jumeau towards the door, as if, beyond that threshold, lay secrets and darkness. 'The uncertainty of it all, Jumeau,' he said flatly. 'The uncertainty of it all.'

'Very well,' said Jumeau.

'Before we start, might I have a glass of water?'

'Some water?'

'Yes. From the faucet would be fine.'

'Of course.'

Jumeau went to the bedside table and opened the cupboard door. He fell to his knees and peered into the darkness. To his surprise, at the back of the cupboard, a tall, clean glass caught what little light had sneaked into the shadows and winked. He did not recall the glass. At best he had hoped for a filthy mug that would have to be scraped of any wildlife within. Jumeau reached in and grabbed it.

'I have a glass,' he said triumphantly.

'Clean, I hope,' said Wint.

'That I have a glass at all comes as a surprise, Mr Wint.'

Light poured through the glass, refracted and fell upon Jumeau's wrist as a rainbow. It had not collected a single speck of dust during its time in the recesses of his bedside table. It appeared unused, new even.

'I'll get some water.'

He went across the hallway to the bathroom. The dingy room stank of summer damp, the kind of damp that leaked from hidden pipes and lay festering beyond the walls until it was ripe enough to take on a life of its own and begin to eat away at the foundations. He turned on the cold faucet. The water came out strong and clear and had the icy glint of a mountain waterfall. Jumeau could not remember the water ever being so certainly cold, so ideally clear and the flow so purposefully strong. It made him want to drink it, to swim in it. He filled the glass and drank. The water fell across his tongue like a fresh tide sent to wash away the debris from the weed strewn beach. It hit the back of his throat with the welcome ferocity of an icy pool on a hot summer day as you broke the surface of the water and felt it embrace your skin, inch by inch, until you were submerged weightless in its cool grasp. He felt the water slide down his chest, leaving a cold burn as it went, until it fell into his stomach and made him feel as if he glowed a refreshing blue from within. He drank the entire glass with a pleasure he had never known in a simple glass of water and was almost tempted to take another when he remembered Wint. He refilled the glass and took it back to his room. He put the glass down on the floor in the shade so that it would not warm up, then took the Dansette off its small table, put the table next to Wint and placed the glass dead centre on the table. Condensation rolled down the outside of the glass and pooled at its base.

'Your water, Mr Wint.'

'Thank you,' said Wint. He picked up the glass and took a sip then, finding it pleasant, took a longer drink until the glass was half empty. For the first time, in the centre of Wint's bald, pale head, Jumeau saw a fat drop of sweat. It rolled slowly, thickly, towards the part of his head that was in the sun and disappeared. 'I am ready now,' said Wint as he replaced the glass.

'Very well,' said Jumeau. He returned to the easel and began to mix paints. His eyes flitted from the sketch, to Wint and back to the canvas in an eternal triangle.

He wasn't sure, but the chair seemed somehow larger today that yesterday. Was it possible that, as well as losing some of his wounds, Wint had shed some of his weight?

'May I take you to dinner?' Wint contrived to fashion his tie as he spoke.

'Yes,' said Jumeau.

Wint paused only for a second, then carried on with his tie. 'What do you like to eat?'

Jumeau honestly did not know. Neither did he know why he had said yes, and so quickly, to Wint's request. 'How about I leave the choice to you? I'm sure you have better knowledge of such things than I do and know the better places.'

'Indeed I do,' said Wint, apparently happy with Jumeau's decision. He slipped on his jacket. 'Do you have any other clothes?' he asked casually.

Jumeau looked down at is paint-flecked jeans and T-shirt. 'I might have a pair of trousers and a knitted shirt somewhere,' he lied. 'It hadn't occurred to him that his comfort clothes caused discomfort in others.

'Good, said Wint. He prodded a finger towards Jumeau's chest and followed a line of red paint from his neck to his crotch. Jumeau thought it quite pretty against the other spatters that had gathered over time, the result of more than one moment or artistic extravagance, but realised that it would probably not be acceptable in any establishment frequented by the debonair Mr Wint.

'Do you like crab?' asked Wint.

'I do,' said Jumeau with unusual gusto. Food was not usually of too much interest to him. 'It has always been a favourite of mine, but I haven't had it for many years, finances being as they are...' He trailed away, embarrassed by the admission.

'Then we shall do crabs and expensive wine and anything else that takes our fancy,' said Wint.

If he was honest, Jumeau felt a little uneasy about the whole idea and wondered if it was possible to retract his impulsive 'yes'. What on earth had possessed him? Holly perhaps. He had certainly enjoyed his time with her and regretted its passing in an almost mournful way. Was it possible that she had opened him up to possibilities? He had been afraid that it would be Wint who would infect him with need, with realisation. Maybe it was. If he hadn't spent time with Wint then he might not have been so bloody talkative in the diner...he thought of her firm abdomen and hazelicious eyes and of the glimpses he had caught of her pudenda and they sat upon the sill. What wouldn't he give for another night with her? He dragged his mind back. So Wint had led to Holly who had led to Wint and with each meeting his wall had cracked a little more and he had been able to take in the fresh air and sunlight that crept between the bricks and found that he liked it. That was why he had said yes, because Wint had awoken something in him that he had thought long-dead – curiosity. He had given up looking for more because he had believed that there was no more, at least no more that was good. He had retreated behind his wall with his ears and eyes covered and his mouth gagged by the glue of uncertainty and fear.

'Why?' he asked Wint.

'Oh, purely selfish motives, dear boy. I happen to like crab and expensive wine.'

'No,' said Jumeau. 'Why the meal?'

Wint tutted. 'Because life is for living,' he snapped, as if the answer was too obvious and really too beneath him to be worthy of utterance.

'I have lived my life satisfactorily,' said Jumeau defensively.

'Not mine, you haven't,' said Wint sharply. 'I shall return at seven and we shall drive along the coast to the finest seafood restaurant I know and we shall bedeck ourselves with bibs and drown ourselves in ice-cold champagne and buttery luxury.' He opened the door. 'Seven sharp,' he warned with an almost smile. 'And I am never late.'

'I'll be ready,' said Jumeau.

He stood with his hands on his hips and shook his head. What the hell? He could feel that black cloud of terror and regret begin to absorb him, but he also felt a scurry of excitement in his solar plexus at the prospect of leaving, albeit temporarily, the prison sanctuary of the four walls in which he had for so long voluntarily immured himself.

He went over to the bed and got down on his knees. Underneath the bed, among the dust-bunnies and strings of web, he could see the outline of an old suitcase. He lay on his stomach and stretched out an arm beneath the bed. His fingers grasped the handle of the case and dragged it towards him. It bulldozed through the thick layer of dust so that, as it came closer, the dust became a giant grey wave that roiled and writhed across the wooden floor.

Jumeau picked up the case and laid it upon the bed. It was a nice case, or had been once upon a time, all chagrin and brown leather and fine, tight stitching. As he opened the lid, the two catches still able to deliver a satisfyingly solid clunk as the spring mechanism threw them up and away, a mat of dust slid onto the bed. It had been so long since he had slid the case beneath the bed that he had no recollection of what was inside it. He had taken everything he needed - pants, socks, shirts - out of it when he had moved in and hidden the case in the only place available. The landlady had said that he could store things in a cupboard in the hallway, but he didn't trust people enough to leave things at the mercy of others. Upon opening it, he was surprised to see that it was still three-quarters full. It was also completely dust-free and everything inside appeared to be as neatly arranged as the day it had been packed. Jumeau was pleased and surprised to see, at the top of the pile, a good-as-new dark green knitted shirt. He lifted it out of the case and held it up to the light. He had no memory of it, not of buying it or packing it so carefully into the case. Beneath that was a pair of cream slacks, also seemingly unused. They were good ones too, sharply creased and already with a sturdy leather belt around the waist. He laid the shirt and the trousers carefully across the back of the chair in which Wint had sat, then returned to the case. On impulse, he decided that he would empty it. Rarely in life was there a greater temptation than a forgotten box. He would empty it and lay the contents out across the bed. Who knew what treasures he would find within? Before he did so, he put the case back onto the floor and, in a single swift movement, swept the bedclothes into his arms and carried them into a dark corner where he dropped them. What remained was a mattress that had seen better days. Down the middle of it was a trough, that same trough into which he rolled each night and, with an effort, out of which he rolled each morning. It had, over the years, become heavily stained. He had inherited it from the previous owner, possibly several previous owners, and was therefore happy to say that not all the exudates had been his. It was however quite thick upon the material of the mattress, as if someone had died and melted into it. He supposed that to be entirely possible. He considered turning it over, looked beneath it, concluded that there was little difference and let it fall back into place. The springs beneath hummed inharmoniously as the heavy mattress flopped back into place.

Satisfied that he could do no more, he returned the case to the bed. He removed firstly two more 'as-new' knitted tops, a red one and a black one, followed by a pair of navy slacks. Beneath those were two pairs of canvas shoes, one navy, one black. He shook his head continuously as he discovered and then removed the clothes and placed them in a neat pile on the cleanest area of the bed. He found socks and underwear and they too ended up in a small pile next to the shirts and pants.

Then he came upon an envelope, roughly torn open, so that it looked as if it was baring its teeth and daring him to plunge his fingers inside. He picked it up and turned it over. He recognised the writing as belonging to his wife. It had the large loops, angular letters and descending drift of a serial killer. It turned his stomach. His first thought was to destroy it, to tear it up into smaller and smaller pieces, put it in an ashtray and watch it burn, then ceremonially tip the ashes from his window and let the hot spirals of air transport them to wherever fate deemed they should rest. He was tempted to throw it back into the case and bury it beneath clothing or simply screw it into a tight ball and lob it into the bin, but he held onto it, sat on the edge of the bed and turned it over in his hands. He sniffed at it. The residue of her perfume still lingered and mingled with the smell of aged paper. She liked her perfume, did Anne-Marie. Had they ever had kids, they probably would have been born stinking of Chanel, she had absorbed so much of the stuff. His thumbs took it upon themselves to sneak into the raggedy mouth of the envelope and reveal the folded leaves of thin, violet-tinted notepaper. She had possessed stationery for every occasion it seemed, even for cuckolding. Was that something specific you could buy or could you adapt any notepaper into cuckolding paper?

He knew full well what the envelope contained. It was the death certificate of their marriage, the confirmation that it had finally come to an end after a long period of suffering. The cause of death? Exhaustion. Contributing factors? Heart failure, for sure, inflammation of the brain, without doubt, bad humours and a simple failure to thrive.

He took out the notepaper and laid the envelope aside. He opened the paper and found to his surprise that it was just a single sheet. The way it had been folded led him to believe that it was more substantial, that the life and death of a marriage would be worth more than a single, thin piece of paper. He opened it carefully and held it between the thumb and forefinger of each hand. He could feel the dampness pass between the tips of his fingers and the delicate paper and imagined that his acidic sweat had already burned a hole through it.

Did he really want to read this? Did he really want to relive the dying moments? Did he really want the truth? Yes. Yes he did. And he knew that there was a truth in there somewhere, even if it wasn't his.

He rested the paper on his knees and lowered his eyes. As he saw her writing, he could hear her tense, rhotic, Mid-Atlantic tone.

Jumeau (it began),

I have gone. I will not return. I have chosen to be reborn in the arms of Johnson White, the cripple from the car showroom. He may be withered, but he is still more complete than you will ever be. You have brought to me nothing but pain and disappointment. You cannot hold down a job. You have no friends. You hate the world for no more reason than that it has the gall to exist. I don't know if you can paint. I wouldn't know a good painting from a bad, all I know is that you persist in this fantasy that it somehow matters. It does not. You have stopped living and you expect me to do the same. You love yourself more than anything in the world and expect me to do the same. I can never love you that much. The more I have got to know you, the further my love for you has diminished. The more distant you have become, the safer I have begun to feel. You are the most selfish, self-absorbed, inconsiderate man I have ever met, and I will include my brother Michael in that, and he is a son-of-a-bitch. You should have married him. Johnson loves me. His lopsided sex has more passion than your one-sided piggybacking ever did. You are not a bad man, Jumeau, despite all I say. You are just so indifferent towards all the things that you are supposed to love and so full of vitriol for things you don't even know. An artist should see the beauty in things. I don't hold with this new-fangled idea that you have to put your soul on display for your work to have any value. Pollock is an asshole. His self-indulgent spitting that you so admire is no more than the posset of a spoiled and overfed child, but what the hell do I know? This letter might seem to you to be the outpourings of a bitch, no more. Some of it might well be, but mostly it's a lament for my love. I loved you, Jumeau, down to the last drop of blood that flowed through my breaking heart. I took you on because I thought I could reign you in, change you and still get the same thrill from the dangers I saw twinkle in those hard, grey eyes of yours. I was wrong. I was wrong to try to change you, to expect you to change, to expect the thrill to remain once I had your balls in my bag. This is as much my fault as it is yours. I will not ask you for money or any form of settlement. I came to you with nothing and am content to leave with nothing (except for my perfumes and china pieces). You are a man of many rooms, Jumeau, each of them closed off from the others so that there is never any conflict within or without. You keep your feelings stored in unopened boxes that lie dusty upon the floors of these rooms and, unless you are willing to open them, I fear that you will always be alone and fear that you think this the right way to be. It is not. I wish you happiness, Jumeau, God knows, I really do, but somehow I think your idea of happiness and mine are just worlds apart.

Goodbye and good luck,

Anne-Marie.

Jumeau stared at the letter. He must have read it before and yet he remembered none of it. It seemed to him that his marriage had not died of natural causes, it had been murdered and he was culpable. His memory had served him differently and done him a disservice. She was right in all she wrote. He was selfish. He was self-absorbed. He *was* a man of many rooms. He should have seen the interconnectedness of all things instead of bundling them into their dark and dusty compartments where they would at best remain meaningless and, at worst, fester like an unhealed infection, ready to one day erupt or, maybe even worse than that, to never erupt, but simply bubble and rumble and upset the delicate balance of heart and mind. They all had their own rooms; mother, father, lover, wife, next door to failures and successes and hopes and fears and, in isolation, all they did was damage a man. Together, in all their colours, they made the man, if only the man had been willing to set them free.

He folded the letter back up, making sure to keep to the folds already there, and slipped it back into the envelope. What was she doing now? Was she happy? Were she and Johnson White happy? He hoped so. He hoped that the man with the withered leg had given her everything that the man with the withered heart had been unable to.

He tucked the envelope away between some shirts. He found a photo and picked it up, turned it towards the light so that the monochrome was tinged with the gold of a late afternoon. At first, he didn't recognise the two happy-go-lucky youngsters on the boardwalk, then realised that it was him and Anne-Marie. Jeez, she was really beautiful. He had remembered her as sour-faced, all angles and tight lips. The truth of it was that she still had the fat of youthful innocence in her face and the light of hope in her eyes. Her dark hair fell upon her shoulders, draped across the top of her breasts, and her figure was the figure of one who, at that point, was happy with their life. And she smiled. He could not remember her ever smiling, but the evidence was before him now. She had been a beautiful, ordinary girl and that was probably more than any man had a right to ask for. He shouldn't simply have held onto her; he should have made her *want* to stay, but there she was now, in a room of her own, only just now coming out blinking into the light of his new reality. He ran a thumb across her face as if he could absorb his wrongs, could stain his skin with the new-found reminder of her goodness. He put the photo inside the envelope and tucked it away again between the shirts.

That was it, all that the case had to yield. It was enough. It was a new continent discovered, a new part of the main, a part of himself, an interconnection, despite himself.

12

Jumeau awoke to feel a warm breeze upon his face. Beneath that, the sun, not quite ready to surrender the world to its sister moon, still played hotly upon his skin. He kept his eyes closed. He wasn't falling, he knew that, despite the rush of air around him. He could smell the sea. It was a salty, sour smell, infused with the sweet heat of roadside flowers and, he was sure, a man's perfume. To his left he could hear the hollow growl of an engine as it bounced off a wall. So, he thought to himself, to the left the cliffs, to the right, the sea. If it hadn't been for the sound of the engine, he might have been flying, a gull gliding free along the edge of the world, above the perpetual white line that divided sea and land.

'You're awake are you?'

Jumeau opened his eyes. He squinted in the light of the lowering sun.

'Your breathing changed,' said Wint. 'A sudden surge of consciousness.'

Jumeau rubbed his eyes. 'Where are we?'

'Along the coast road. On our way to crustacean Heaven.'

Jumeau lifted his head. He found himself in the passenger seat of a gorgeous, elegant Mercedes-Benz 190SL. The paintwork was gunmetal grey, the seats sumptuous red leather. He turned his head lazily towards Wint. He was playing the part – sunglasses, white scarf flicking at the breeze, leather driving gloves, navy blazer and cream slacks. He wore a hat that near as dammit made him captain of the ship. Jumeau thought he looked dapper. Yes, that was the word – dapper. The nude man with scars who sat motionless at his window, was dapper. D...A...double P...E...R. He turned his head to the sea. The light was end-of-day golden and fell upon the darkening sea like pieces of eight. Bay horses rode the waves and threw themselves suicidally upon the sand. On the horizon, the silhouettes of ships lay like a slow moving city while about them the sky slipped away with the slow demise of day. Blue-eyed gannets dive-bombed the sea in a final desperate search for a day's-end snack beneath the thick waters. It was a great time, this time of the turning of the tide, when there was no day, no night, just a crepuscular no-man's-land where past and future blended seamlessly and existence was all just a holding of the breath until the giant sigh of night shed the past and brought the future crashing down.

'How did I get here?' asked Jumeau, his eyes still on the gentle swells and the slowly bruising sky.

Wint changed down as the car approached a stubborn bend. His feet were surprisingly quick as he read the road perfectly and he depressed the clutch, accelerated out of the bend and then moved swiftly into top gear.

'How do you think you got here, dear boy? It's all that concentration, you know. All that energy expended focusing on one thing for such a long time. It exhausts the mind. You fell asleep almost as soon as we pulled away.'

Jumeau looked at his clothes. He had on the green knitted top, cream trousers and navy canvas shoes that he had intended and yet could not recall putting them on. 'I must have been very tired,' he said, although it had really only been a thought out loud.

'I'm sure you were,' said Wint above the engine and the wind that dipped and dived about them. 'Anyway, a bit of shut-eye will have done you good. You don't want to be nodding off with a crab claw in your fist and butter on your chin, do you? Nearly there now. Couple more miles. Smoke if you wish. I'm not one of those precious fellows who won't let people have fun in their cars.'

Jumeau patted himself down and found two packs of Chesterfields, one in each deep pocket, and some matches. They were each brand new, even the matches. He smiled to himself. He really must have been tired if he didn't remember putting these in his pockets. He slit open a pack, lit one and tossed the match towards the blurred tongue of road just a few inches beneath them. He put his head back against the soft leather. The cow had not died in vain. This was good. This was all so good; the feel of clean air upon his face, the last tendrils of sun, the sense of freedom, freedom announced by the sound of a fine, powerful, sleek engine and beneath that the forlorn cry of gulls and the distant whisper of the surf as it fingered its way to the shoreline and died in a flurry of bubbles.

The Mercedes rounded a final bend, devouring the tarmac with unhindered joy and then pulled into the parking lot of a beaten up shack that was all peeled yellow paint and dry, split wood. Wint turned the engine off and they both sat and listened as the car ticked and tutted and sighed as it cooled in the gentle caress of the sea breeze.

'Here we are,' said Wint with a thunderous clap of his fleshy hands. 'Don't worry about how it looks. That's all part of the charm. Come on, let's go and get some fizz inside us and half a hundred weight of crab.' He slapped Jumeau playfully on the thigh and bundled himself giddily out of the car.

Who was this man? wondered Jumeau. What a difference. What a fantastic difference. It was as if they had known each other all their lives, as if this friendship was the most natural thing in the world. He jumped out of the car. Now he could look down upon the sea properly, over the beach grass and onto the sands that rippled in the wake of a thousand wind snakes, which slithered across its grainy belly and reshaped it with every breath; down towards the water's edge, where land and sea melted into one another like lovers in a hurried moment of ecstasy before dying entwined; down towards the vast expanse of the sea itself, the waters of which were a kaleidoscope of colours, as if someone had melted the sky like a pot of crayons and poured it carefully onto the meniscus of the sea. A hundred yards off shore, no more than a grey silhouette, a man sat in a small boat and fished. He must have been at such peace, amid a carpet of many colours. Jumeau imagined the man to have sharp blue eyes set in a hard, brown, weather-beaten skin, with crow's feet gained from smiling in absolute contentment with his lot in this world.

He followed Wint to the front of the shack across dusty ground chewed on by pebbles as people walked along and the wind as it whipped along impatiently on darker days and winter nights. The front of the shack faced the sea. It was as weather-worn and salt-bitten as the rest of the shack, while two large windows reflected the closing curtains of sea and land like two giant eyes casting a final sad look upon the passing day.

Wint passed through the main door that was propped open by a giant seashell, its outside encrusted with knots of hard white calcium, the smooth, orange-pink inside as ripe and soft as any skin. The place was dimly lit, not so dim that you couldn't see anything or to cast gloom, but not so bright as to steal the stunning view from the natural light of the sky and sea. Wint picked a window table and sat down. Jumeau followed his lead. It looked darker outside than it actually was due to the glass and the internal lighting. The sunset colours were heightened so that all was just a mass of broken, rainbow-infused mirror. This was as he imagined the end of the universe to be, as the final day slid away to be replaced by a silent, starry void.

'Sometimes,' he said, 'I would go somewhere, you know, to sketch or paint, and I found that I couldn't because what I saw was just so beautiful that I just stood there and wept because nothing I could do, nothing, could ever capture and hold that beauty, that moment, that absolute perfection. I was beaten. It made me redundant. It turned my stomach until I thought I would throw up and I had to leave, to turn my back on it, pretend that it was just a dream, that it was never really there. So, I returned to the ordinary, the bland, the safe. I denied that beauty because, if I didn't it would kill me.' He lit a cigarette and placed the packet of Chesterfields upon the table and the box of matches on top of them. He drew upon it long and hard and barely felt the thick smoke enter his lungs. Maybe at last he was becoming immune to their effect. 'Do you understand what I mean, Mr Wint?'

Wint frowned. 'I am shallow, Jumeau. If I don't understand it, I ignore it. I appreciate beautiful things, but I do not live by them and I would most certainly not die by them.'

A girl in an orange skirt, white blouse and flat black shoes came over to them. She had a smile switched on and a bounce in her walk. She reminded Jumeau of Holly.

'Help you?'

'Yes,' said Wint. 'Champagne in fresh...' he raised a finger, '*fresh* ice. We'll take the blue crab by the bucket load, a side order of fries and some heavily buttered bread. White bread, not that brown muck.'

The girl scrawled the order down. 'Sure. I'll be back in two tics with your champagne.' She looked at each of them with smiling eyes and lips. Jumeau returned the smile and hoped that she did not take offence at Wint's bluntness. He had heard that staff would spit into the food of rude customers, even urinate. He did not want to have come this far to have to watch out for bubbles of spit on his food or have his crab distinguished by that unwashed, boiled kidney smell reminiscent of hospital kitchens and cheap dining halls. The girl left.

'How goes the masterwork?' asked Wint.

Jumeau nodded reflectively. 'Good. I think you'll be pleased with it. I should only need you tomorrow and then I'll just need a day or two to round off the rough edges.'

'You work quickly,' said Wint appreciatively.

'I didn't have to worry about the clothes. That always helps.' Jumeau smiled.

The champagne arrived in a deep bucket littered with diamonds of ice.

'Do you think it odd, that I should ask to be painted in the nude, with my affliction?'

'I hadn't thought about it.'

'Really?'

Jumeau shook his head. 'Not the actual nudity, no. I thought about the scars. I wondered how you lived with them, especially appearing as they do. I thought...I actually thought that you were quite brave to expose yourself; either that or exceptionally vain.'

Wint poured them each a glass of champagne. The golden liquid bubbled audibly into a pair of fine and expensive flutes. Light passed through them and fell in golden drops upon the table. This was clearly, thought Jumeau, much more than a shack by the sea. The champagne was dry and refreshing and it was all Jumeau could do to stop himself downing the glass in one, but he didn't want to. Habit demanded it of him, but he wanted to taste the wine, the soil from which the grapes came, the sunshine and sweet rain upon which they had fed, the *liqueur de triage*, that blend of sugar, wine and yeast that launched the champagne into that second explosive fermentation and then the time spent *en pupitre*, where the bottles lay head down until one of the wandering gods, hands in pockets and legs set to saunter, decided that the time was right to release it upon the world. He wanted to feel the coldness and the bubbles and the crisp dryness. He wanted to *enjoy* it, not need it. He did not feel the need to blunt the edge because, for some reason, there was no edge to blunt, just an overwhelming desire to savour, to savour everything.

'I am vain,' said Wint. 'We are all vain, the only difference is the depth of the vanity, and there lies my only depth, but it wasn't vanity that was behind the idea of being painted in the nude.' He paused in thought and, as usual, all the thought lay in his charged emerald eyes while his face remained unchanged, no matter the disturbances and the turmoil behind it. 'I have never shown my scars, Jumeau. Not to anyone. Not even to my mother, God rest her. They have prevented intimacy on any normal level. Even those whom I have paid for sex have been repulsed by my wounds. So I have poured everything I have into my shallowness. My scars have ensured a life without depth, without real love, without the...steadiness for which we all search. And the greatest irony of all is that they are now beginning to heal, just as I am beginning to die.'

13

Jumeau was at a loss for words. His mind and jaw were dislocated, both limp and useless. How absurdly unreal things had just become.

As he stared at him, Wint flinched and grabbed his flank, as if he had been shot. He put his hand beneath his jacket. When he pulled it out, it was smeared with blood. Wint saw the horror upon Jumeau's face. 'It's okay,' he said. 'It'll go as quickly as it came.' He picked up a thick cloth napkin, folded it roughly and placed it beneath his shirt, directly upon the wound. 'The one that happened in your apartment didn't even leave a scar.' He smiled. For the first time a dimple appeared at the side of his mouth and Jumeau noticed that there were creases at the sides of his eyes. 'Bloody thing hurt too. It owed me a scar at the very least.'

He suddenly laughed and the creases around his eyes deepened. The laugh continued, a soft bark that grew in frequency and volume until it became so forceful that Wint's shoulders began to roll and the rest of his huge body followed in a chain reaction until it too shuddered violently in his seat. His deep bark became the only sound in the place. It drowned all other noises. The tinkling of cutlery disappeared and the other diner's voices became submerged. Their hands moved across their plates mechanically and their mouths, silent, dark pits in the centre of meaninglessly animated faces, formed empty shapes, their elastic lips stretched to white thinness or puckered to crimson, leech-like fatness as they made pointless gestures to the one opposite them. None of them seemed to have heard Wint, seemed to notice the vacuum that his laugh had created.

Jumeau watched dumbfounded as the faults of humanity began to etch themselves into Wint's skin. Before his eyes he aged five years, ten, fifteen as, with each roll of his body, Wint's face began to develop the trenches and furrows that came with the wars and workings of a normal life and he began to take on the shape of someone who had lived, who had a skull and blood vessels and nerve endings beneath that once puffy, pale flesh. Life itself was beginning to come to life upon Wint.

Jumeau became afraid. His impulse was to flee, but to where? He didn't even really know where he was, except that he was on the coast road south.

'Mr Wint!' he whispered harshly. 'Mr Wint!'

Wint did not stop. His barked laugh consumed all. It bounced off the windows and walls and ceiling and echoed around him in sharp, fractured shards, filled Jumeau's head until he thought that it would burst at the sutures, those inherently weak points of the skull, that had fused so long ago.

'Mr Wint!' he shouted. He put a hand upon Wint's hand. It was ice cold, bloodless. 'Mr Wint!'

Everything stopped. People froze and stared at him and Wint's eyes, those emerald eyes, burned into Jumeau's eyes with the ferocity of lasers. All was silence. Wint no longer laughed. His face was frozen, his mouth stuck in a rictus, his eyes wide, his eyebrows arched, his once smooth pale skin now etched with the sallow decrepitude of age. People no longer scraped knives and forks on plates or sucked the moist and tender meat from the hard corpses laid before them. Their mouths were closed, their lips pursed, as they stared intently at the one who had brought their moment to a juddering halt.

'Yes?' said Wint as he looked down at his companion's hand laid across his own. 'What is it, dear boy?'

Instantly, the room came to life again, as if Wint's question had somehow reignited life. He looked sympathetically at Jumeau, his face creased with concern, his sharp eyes now somehow suddenly dulled by the sediment of age.

'I'm sorry,' stuttered Jumeau. 'I just wanted to say how sorry I am, about you dying. How long have you known?'

'I found out a couple of days before I saw you. That was what prompted me to find you.'

Jumeau gazed at Wint. He had become thinner, his shirt collar like a trench around his neck, his jacket loose about the once full, round shoulders. 'Isn't there anything anyone can do?'

'We can drink champagne and eat crab, Jumeau. We can take the coast road at sunset and wonder at the turning of the earth and know that it will still turn after we are gone. All we can do is accept the moment and treat it as a lifetime.' He emptied his glass and encouraged Jumeau to do the same, then refilled them. 'And ask someone to forgive us our sins.'

A harsh laugh exploded from Jumeau. 'Our sins? No, no, no, Mr Wint. There is no forgiveness because there are no sins. There is what you do and what you don't do, that is all. There is no God, no nirvana, no rebirth, no Heaven, no Hell. There are just the worms or the flames.' He suddenly realised that he was talking, ranting, to a dying man. Surely he should be offering comfort, not truth. 'I'm sorry...'

'Don't be. It's not about me, but I still need to be forgiven.'

'Fine. I forgive you.' Jumeau drew a cross upon the air. '*In nomine patris et filii et spiritus sancti.*' He dropped his hand. 'There. Consider yourself absolved.' Jumeau felt ashamed of his flippancy, but what else could he do in the face of such absurdity? Such *absurdity*.

'Absolved for what?' pressed Wint.

'For everything. For every illicit copulation, for all that you have stolen, for all that you have envied, for your jealousies and your greed, for your idleness and your idolatry. I forgive you for drinking too much, for thinking too much, for every bad thought and every bad deed.' He lit a Chesterfield. He was shaking angry. He had not been this way for so many years. Damn him! Damn the man! What did he want from him? If *he* had done all those things, then he would not crave absolution because there was no absolution to be had. All you could do was drag your sins or misdeeds or whatever they should be called, to the grave and let them be buried with you. If they lived on in others, then that was fine, they could carry the weight. 'Is that it? Is that enough?' He didn't sound angry. He even managed a thin smile.

The girl brought their crab to the table. It looked like someone had simply emptied the sea before them. Next to the crab she placed two large bowls of melted butter.

'There we go gentlemen,' said the girl. 'Crab, fries and heavily buttered *white* bread.' She smiled disarmingly at Wint, who almost returned the smile. 'Will there be anything else?'

'Pop another bottle in that ice would you, dear?'

The waitress tilted her head. 'Of course.'

When she had left, Wint's eyes smothered the table in greedy love. 'Are you *au fait* with eating these things? It's just hammer and grab really or, if you are particularly impatient, hammer and suck.'

'I'm fine,' said Jumeau.

He picked up a thick claw and tapped at it with the small heavy hammer until it split neatly down the centre. He pulled the two halves apart then gently teased the meat from inside, dipped it into the hot melted butter and passed it dripping into his mouth. It was exquisite. Beyond exquisite. It was velvet food, soft and luxurious. He had thought that the butter would simply layer his mouth in grease and leave him with an unpleasant, claggy feeling, but with a wash of the cold champagne, the whole went down effortlessly and left him longing for more.

'And the child?' asked Jumeau. 'You said that you had killed a child. Is that included in the package or would it require a more meaningful blessing, a more thorough scourging? A sprinkle of blessed holy champagne, perhaps. Unless you were making it up, of course.'

Wint put his hand beneath his shirt and pulled out the napkin he had used to staunch the bleeding from his fresh wound. It was like a damp, newly tie-dyed cloth. He regarded it disdainfully and dropped it into the ice bucket. The blood leeched from the cloth and billowed into the freezing water, turning it rose. He put his hand back to the wound, then checked his palm and fingers, saw that there was no fresh blood, rearranged his clothing and helped himself to more crab.

'I was not making it up, Jumeau.' There was no sense of confrontation or resentment in his voice, merely a statement of fact. 'I did kill a child, but I think you already know that to be true. You know me very well.'

'I'm not sure that I know you at all, Mr Wint. When? When did this happen?'

Wint continued to eat as if he was simply recounting the tale of an incident at some traffic lights that he had observed from a distance. He slurped a piece of crab into his mouth and wiped his hands on his napkin. 'Korea. You would think that we would have had enough of wars by then but, no, we had to stick our finger into another pie and away we went again to the other side of the world to fight for God knows what in a place which I'm pretty sure God had never heard of. Would you like to hear the tale? I warn you, it might be the ruination of a perfect evening.'

'Go ahead,' said Jumeau. 'I am able to separate the one from the other.' Wasn't that what his wife

had said, not in so many words, but essentially that?
A man of many rooms? So many of them locked?

Wint wiped a trail of butter from his chin and
took a large gulp of champagne. As he tipped his head
back, Jumeau saw that his neck had become ragged, a
normal, ragged, turkey neck of a normal ragged man.
His chin was now sharply visible instead of lying
dormant beneath a layer of flesh.

'I was,' said Wint, '- how shall I say it?- co-
opted into the infantry in fifty-one. Believe it or not,
back then I was quite a skinny beau of a boy. I had
recently finished a degree at university and was eager
to get out there, into the world. I had a job waiting
for me, in advertising. Then in January fifty-one, I
was called up and by August I was in Gangwon
Province in South Korea.' He cracked open another
claw, dipped it in one of the bowls of butter, and
sucked the meat from the shell. 'On August 18, the
Battle of Bloody Ridge began. You might be aware of
it?'

'I've heard of it,' said Jumeau.

'Of course you have. It lasted two and a half
weeks and was fought in deep mud and even deeper
fear. Two and a half thousand allies died. Fifteen
thousand on the other side. I have never been so
scared in my life.' His eyes took on a life of their own
as they delved into the secret history that lay hidden,
buried, deeply behind them. 'It was just explosion

after explosion after explosion. The air was filled with the stench of burning; burning trees, burning buildings, burning people. When you breathed, you breathed in a residue of what had been incinerated beneath our shells. There was nowhere to go for clean air. You could get close to the ground, into the mud and roll about in the filth, but even then, a fine powder settled upon the mud and ended up in your ears, your nose, your mouth, your eyes. I might have ingested an entire human being for all I know. Anyway, as with all these things, when an immovable object meets an immovable object, we got closer to each other, like tectonic plates grinding, causing the ground to vibrate until, one day, we saw each other face to face and went in hand to hand.'

Jumeau lit a cigarette. Wint's face was decaying before his eyes. It was as if all the moisture was being sucked from his skin and, as it left, it left its own Bloody Ridge in the lines around his eyes, the furrows on his forehead, in the deep scythes around his mouth. Even his eyes, those jewels, those shining emeralds, seemed to have dulled, to have lost their greenness and were gradually fading towards a monochrome, a grey, a grey that looked like storm clouds on some distant horizon.

'I was blind,' continued Wint. 'I was blind with fear and rage and confusion. I shot and stabbed and kicked and punched my way forward, screaming in anticipation of the inevitable pain to come, screaming for mercy, screaming out of fear, but never screaming out of bravado.' He smiled forlornly. 'I simply had none. I found myself with my hands wrapped around someone's throat and I was just squeezing, in the same way that you would wring a cloth dry. I could feel whoever was in my hands kicking me, punching me, but it had no effect, like throwing tiny pebbles at an elephant. Then they stopped, not all at once, but gradually. The kicks and punches just became weaker, flailed in hope and in vain rather than with any accuracy. Then they stopped and I knew that they were dead. I knew because they became heavy. I could feel their weight in my hands. Then my sight came back and I saw them and I realised that I had throttled a child. The North Koreans denied it, but we had heard that they were using child soldiers and this proved it, this rag doll in his pathetic, tiny uniform. I dropped the child and he fell and when he hit the ground he was shapeless, an arm here, a leg there, his neck just...wrong. I don't know how old he was, twelve, maybe thirteen, not old enough to jerk off or drive a car or have a beer, just old enough to die. I killed two more children that day. I know that for sure because I used my pistol and I paid particular attention to where my bullets went after I had strangled that poor child. It was easier with the pistol. There was more distance, so I couldn't smell them or feel the softness of their flesh or see the shine in their black hair or the colour of their eyes or think of their mothers and their fathers and their sisters and brothers and the empty bedroom that would forever be a shrine to a wasted life.' He picked up another crab claw and rolled it absently through his fingers. 'When I told you that I had killed a child, Jumeau, I wasn't boasting. I was confessing. It had nothing to do with Heaven or Hell or reincarnation, it was just an emptying of the sump, to make room for more waste.' He idly tossed the crab claw back among the other claws. 'Can you forgive me? I've always thought that the right thing to do would have been to die out there, to let the children live, or at least leave the killing to someone else. But, you see, I wanted to live. I wanted to live more than I wanted the children to live. *Can* you forgive me?'

Jumeau pushed his plate away. He'd had enough. He felt fat, bloated and suddenly all the butter he had consumed seemed to ooze from the buds of his tongue and lay thickly in his mouth. He emptied his glass and sluiced his mouth, then poured them each some more of the champagne. 'Of course,' he said, his voice broken. 'Of course I do.'

A tear fell from Wint's eye and rolled through the crags and crannies that made up the cliff of his face. Time had caught up with him. All the wounds and scars had taken their toll. 'Thank you,' he said. He reached into a jacket pocket and took out the car keys. He placed them in the centre of the table and pushed them towards Jumeau. 'The car is yours. The pink slip is in the boot, in the case with ten thousand dollars in it.' He drank his champagne down in one go and sighed. 'I'm going to die now.' He looked at the sea and saw the hot blister of sun balanced upon the horizon, slipping south, dragging the final florid flush of day behind it, followed by the indigo onset of night, then the blackness, punctuated by pinpricks of stars and worlds unknown; forever unknown. He grasped Jumeau's hand. His eyes were full of understanding. 'Be good to yourself, Jumeau. I absolve you. *I* absolve *you*.' His head fell forward onto his chest and with a final slow exhalation, he died.

Jumeau held Wint's hand tightly. 'Mr Wint! Mr Wint! Please...' For all the urgency in his voice, he knew that he could no longer make any difference to Wint.

He looked around the restaurant and saw that no one had noticed. Everybody ate, everybody chatted, everybody drank and laughed and smiled and waltzed in perfect unison across the thin ice of their lives. Waitresses cleared away plates and pirouetted between tables, dashed away crumbs with cloths that swept from their shoulders like wings. They all became a blur, set in a bokeh of tears as Jumeau realised that he had lost Wint.

The waitress came to him. She still smiled and bounced. 'Will there be anything else?'

Jumeau looked from her to Wint and back at her again. 'My friend,' he said. 'He's dead.'

The waitress leaned forward and looked at the top of Wint's head. She put a couple of fingers to his wrist, gazed intently at the watch upon her wrist and said nothing for a full minute. 'He is,' she said eventually. 'He is dead. Would you like to take him away or shall we deal with his leftovers?'

'Are you serious?' What the hell was this? 'He's dead. My friend, my *only* friend, is dead.'

'Would you like to see the manager?'

'What? No. It's not a complaint. I'm just saying, my only friend is dead.'

The waitress continued to smile. 'I see. I appreciate that this is an unexpected end to the evening, but he did warn you, didn't he? He did say that, if he told you that story, that it might be the ruination of a perfect evening, didn't he?'

Jumeau nodded. 'Yes, he did.'

'Well, there you go then.' She bounced gently on the balls of her feet as she waited for Jumeau to react.

'Could I have the bill, please?' asked Jumeau.

'Oh, there's no need for that.' The waitress leaned over and fumbled through Wint's jacket until she found his wallet. She removed it, opened it and extracted some notes, then replaced the wallet. 'He's paid, including a generous gratuity, you might be happy to know.'

'I am,' said Jumeau. 'I am happy. You have been a good waitress.'

'We should have sex,' suggested the waitress.

'We should,' agreed Jumeau.

Without prompting, the waitress removed her white panties and dropped them among the empty crab shells, then squeezed between the chair and the table and straddled Jumeau. She put her hand down and undid his fly. He was hard. She took his penis in her hand and guided it inside her and moved slowly back and forth. Jumeau could feel her hot breath upon his ear. The restaurant fell silent as everyone turned to watch them. Soon, the only sound was their breaths and the soft moans of the waitress as she moved feverishly towards a climax.

'What's your name?' asked Jumeau.

'Table Six,' whispered the girl in his ear. 'Call me Table Six.'

'Table Six,' he said. 'I'm about to come.'

They came together. The other clients watched until they were satisfied that they were both spent, then returned to their food.

Table Six unlatched herself from Jumeau and returned to her place beside the table. 'You're a very good tipper, Monsieur Jumeau,' she said.

'How do you know my name?' he asked as he straightened his clothing.

'It was a guess. Are you going now?'

Jumeau picked up the car keys and his cigarettes and matches. He looked at Wint. He was almost gone now, desiccated, as if a hundred years and a thousand sins had finally caught up with him. 'Yes.'

'He'll be fine,' said Table Six. 'Leave him to us. You just go ahead. I hope that you enjoyed your meal. Drive carefully now.' She smiled the smile and stood unblinkingly before Jumeau.

'Thank you,' he said.

There was no response. With a last look at his friend, he made for the door.

14

Jumeau opened the trunk of the Mercedes. There was nothing in it but a single large brown leather holdall. He leaned in and unzipped the bag. Sure enough it was full of money. Laid on top of the money was the pink slip to the car. He picked it up and tipped it towards the dying light. It was real. It was right. He put it back without touching the money.

So, Wint had known that he would not be leaving he restaurant. He had walked in there, the condemned man, prepared to eat his final meal, ready to die.

Jumeau turned his back on the open trunk and leaned against the car. It was cool now. He could feel the coolness seep through his pants onto the back of his thighs. It was refreshing. The sun had gone and left behind it only a few thin strands of pastel colour. In a few minutes it would be true night. The only sound left was the sound of the sea as it tumbled tiredly onto the shore. All the birds had gone. All the boats had gone. He looked around the parking lot. It was empty. There was only the Mercedes. How was that possible? There must have been fifty people in that shack. He ran through it in his mind, the layout of the tables, the bar, the people at the tables, couples caught in bubbles, friends, lovers, husbands and wives, immersed in each other, the butterfly waitresses flitting between tables with fixed smiles and full hands and skirts that twirled as they turned. He remembered how they stared and how they wrapped themselves in silence as they did so, then reimmersed themselves in a wave of chatter when the silence was dead.

Oh, they were there alright. They were there staring like dogs when he was busy copulating with Table Six, with their greasy chins and stained bibs and unctuous eyes. So where were their cars? How did they get to this Shack-By-the-Sea, this Middle-of-Nowhere, at the side of the south-bound highway, north to south, A to B, with nowhere to stop in between? He lit a cigarette, hung his shoulders as he leaned upon his hands against the car. He stared at the shack and felt his lip start to curl like a dog afraid of ghosts. It sat silently, no more than a silhouette against the indigo sky, all angles and straight lines. The lights were out. Jumeau shivered. The coolness of night caught up with him. He made up his mind and took a step towards the shack. His feet, unfamiliar with the dark uneven ground, kicked up pebbles and dust and felt their wary way over the pot-holed surface. Once, he failed to anticipate a drop, only a couple of inches, and thought he was going down, all the way, forever, to never stop.

He rounded the corner to the front of the shack. It was in darkness. The great fiery eyes that had greeted them were now black and the door was closed. A few feet away, a large shell lay on the ground, home to nothing anymore.

He tried the door. It was locked. He tried again, with force, rattled it until the dried out frame began to shake along with it, but the door did not give. He pressed his face to the glass in the door, cupped his hands around it and squinted at the darkness. There were two red lights, pinpoints, at the far side of the shack. As he focused upon them, they began to move towards him. They floated a few feet above the ground, two intense red dots, level and together. As they came closer, Jumeau could see a shadow form behind them, a meaningless lump of darker emptiness. Then it moved into a patch of yellow moonlight that flared upon the floor and the red dots and meaningless shadow became one, one lithe, thin, muscular, silver-backed beast with rolling shoulders and feet with long claws that tick-tacked against the wooden floor inside the empty, wooden shack.

The wolf stopped six inches from the glass in the door and lowered itself onto its haunches. Its eyes were no longer red, but infused with the creaminess of the moon. Soft white fur masked its eyes and bled into darker fur that thickened into a shiny coat, flecked with silver, at its chest. The top of its head, from just between the eyes, became a trickle of silver, the silver that ran like a river down its back to the beginning of its tail.

Jumeau backed away from the door, his only thought that he could not recall seeing such a magnificent beast inside as he ate his crab and drank his champagne. He was sure he would have noticed, after all, he was an artist, he saw things; that was his job, to see things. This wolf was nearly as tall as him and its thick salt and pepper coat soaked in every spare sliver of light and shone like a grey sea upon a reluctant day. It looked at Jumeau through slightly narrowed eyes, the way a dog will look at its owner in the hope of receiving a titbit at the end of a meal. Jumeau felt no fear, only the curiosity of one who was certain that they had met their killer, their nemesis, the shadow that had stalked them all their life and had now, at last, come into the open to fulfil their destiny.

Jumeau took a step forward, to where he had been before the wolf had floated to the door. He put a hand up to the door handle, long, curved and cold to the touch, and pushed. It was still locked. Without taking its eyes from Jumeau, the wolf lowered its soft muzzle and slowly shook its head. Its long snout drew an invisible arc upon the air. The way was barred, it said. There was no going back. The past had been devoured by the present and the present was already on a plate, ready to sate the future's appetite. Jumeau put his hand flat against the glass. At the same moment, the wolf raised a giant, soft paw and the two connected through the thin glass. Move on, said the wolf. Move on. Take the money, take the car, drive far, drive fast, for the dawn will soon come. Move on.

Jumeau removed his hand. The giant paw fell away. The wolf raised itself, its moonlight eyes level with Jumeau. It walked away, backwards, step by certain step, until the moonlight eyes were turned pale pink and then darkened to blood red dots that floated upon the darkness within the deserted shack.

Jumeau watched the eyes recede until they were gone altogether and once again he was left with nothing but the surf. He realised that he had been crying. He wiped his eyes with his naked fingers and, as he did so, washed away Mr Wint and somehow left himself cleansed.

He put his hands in his pockets and continued to stare through the door into the nothingness beyond.

Had the wolf merely closed its eyes and gone to sleep? Or had it just gone? His eyes lingered and tried to pick out familiar shapes, tables or chairs, but there was nothing to be seen, only the moonlit patch of wooden floor. He turned away and faced the sea. He took a few steps forward and stood at the border of beach grass. In front of him wallowed the syrupy sea, upon which lay the broken moon, which swelled and shrank, swelled and shrank with the rise and tumble of the tide. He looked up to the night sky and saw a billion pinpoint stars. Each one glistened, faded, burst, disappeared, reignited and gave life to the black blanket of sky. He could see Saturn and its slipped halo, the rolling eye of Jupiter, the deep canals and red dust of Mars and the ice-mountains of Pluto. He could see further than he had ever seen and knew with absolute certainty that if he reached out a hand he could break through the gaseous veil of Neptune, dive into the blue and float upon its cloak of winds. He could see it all, from sun to dwarf and beyond and suddenly found himself.

His hand closed around the car keys in his pocket. They jolted him back to reality with their coldness and their sharp edges. The night sky with its billion winking eyes returned. The moon spread its buttery light.

Jumeau took out the keys and walked slowly back to the car. He kicked no stones nor plunged into unseen depths, but took bold and certain steps upon the rocky ground.

When he got to the car, he closed the trunk, then opened the reassuringly heavy driver's door. He sat behind the large black steering wheel and sunk into the red leather seats. The smell of the leather wafted warmly up to his nose and swathed him like a lover or a mother, like someone who cared. He started the ignition and the growl of the engine melded with the purr of the surf and became one. The headlights ate the darkness. He pulled away and the lights swung around, bathed the shack, then left it behind in the shadows.

Jumeau accelerated towards the road, felt the tyres bite into the tarmac and headed up the coast road north.

15

At ninety, the wheels of the Mercedes skimmed the road and only seemed to touch ground when the black snake arched its back. For all Jumeau knew, he was flying. There was darkness to his left and to his right, a vast emptiness through which the coast road ran. The only clue that there was solidity beneath him came from the headlights that reached like fingers into the darkness to point the way. All around him, the breezes eddied and whistled, curled about him like the fingers of an amorous ghost, plucked at his hair, lifted the lapel of his shirt, up and down, up and down, until it buzzed like the wings of a hummingbird, pulled at his skin and narrowed his eyes into the eyes of a killer.

In the distance, he could see the halo of light of the city as it smothered the stars and paled the sky. The road began to descend and now Jumeau saw the polychrome of lights - the cobrahead street lamps that stitched the invisible patchwork of streets together with a weak white light, the buildings, tall and small, that existed only because their jaundiced eyes gawped at the night, the anonymous primaries, from advertising hoardings and jazz clubs and restaurants, that became earthbound stars and flickered through the thick, humid night. It all scalded the landscape, an inflamed, man-made wound that bled the rainbow at night and clotted with the dawn, to spend the day as a grey scab, just waiting for the night to return when its poisons would erupt again and drench the sky in its infected glow.

Jumeau was part of it. He knew that he was as guilty as anybody else out there of shattering the earth. He had helped build the mines where man dug for gold and coal and silver and copper and diamonds and demanded more and more even as there became less and less to give. In a few years, fifty, a hundred, two hundred, it would all be gone and there would be nothing but a pox-ridden planet scarred by the diseased touch of humanity. Man will have ripped the goodness from the earth until there was nothing left but dust. It was human nature to consume, consume, consume, without thought of consequence. It was all now – feed me now, pay me now, give me now, fuck me now; do whatever the hell you want so long as you do it now. Give me the oil. Give me the gas. Give me the fine wooden furniture and the twenty-four ounce steak. Give me a house. Give me electricity. Give me the trinkets and trifles that live by the blue fire which surges through the wires, through our walls and puts cancer in our brains and money in our pockets. Give me a machine to do the work of ten men. Give me a job when the money's spent. Give me a car. Give me a place to bury myself when I'm done and the world is done with me. All the pretty lights were the earth haemorrhaging, an unheeded warning, the beginning of the end, the flame of civilization burning brightly as it died. *What have we done?* Jumeau silently cried. *Oh, God, what have we done? Even as I drive into the Valley of Death, I burn the earth with my beautiful car. I eat the fossil fuels and puke them out and obliterate the sun. What have I done?*

The nose of the Mercedes headed down the long black tongue into the mouth of hell. There were no fires down below, they were all up here, right before our eyes and all we could do was say how pretty they were.

At a hundred miles an hour he broke out of the darkness and into the light. All was a prismatic blur, hazy trails of blue and red and green and yellow, that passed him by like ribbons in the wind.

It took him a moment to notice that he was the only car on the road. It had been expected on the coast road at that time of night. He would have been surprised to have been passed by more than three cars on the entire journey, but he had seen none at all. The streets, the avenues and highways, the side roads and the alleyways were all quiet. Only the sound of his engine as it burbled against the sides of bridges and buildings could be heard. All the lights were on, every shy tiny bulb and each gaudy neon tube; all the office lights gaped blindly across at each other and misted the air between them with a dirty dandelion haze. All the shop fronts burned and spewed their yellow light out onto the sidewalks. All the streetlamps spilled pools of light and stood like whores upon the sidewalks and all the traffic lights switched from red to green and back again, unaware of the changes afoot, determined to go on.

Jumeau slowed to a crawl and took it all in. It was as if the earth had yawned and swallowed the population and left everything else as it was. Eventually nature would reclaim this land and, as each bulb died, so ivy would crawl up the sides of buildings, take root in the metals and the concrete and the glass, and seedlings would take root and bust open the sidewalks and wild flowers would line the highways and shine among the wild grasses and new meadows would be born that stretched from town to town to town, onward forever more.

Jumeau reached a set of lights and stopped. He watched and waited for the passing traffic, as was his habit, for the trucks and cabs and limos and buses and woody wagons that ferried families in high rural style across the treeless plains. Nothing passed. All his senses, those ingrained instincts that humans were not born with but seemed to accumulate with the years, told him to wait. If he nosed himself across the line, then that bus or that giant Mack would come down upon him like a vengeful god and he would be crushed beneath it. No bus came. The lights changed. At the next set of lights, he merely slowed and edged cautiously across. At the next set and all that followed, he simply drove. He had evolved.

There was silence in the city.

He pulled up in the street below his room. Normally he would not have been able to do so, such was the volume of traffic, even at night, but now he could roll to the kerb at his leisure and park. He had considered selling the vehicle as soon as he hit town. He had ten thousand dollars and would get another fifteen hundred at least for the car. He could skip town with the money bag in his hand and buy the first place in the country or by the sea that took his fancy. Hell, he could buy them all. Just get on a bus and go; go far, go fast, go away. He was a rich man now. He turned off the engine and listened. He coughed to reassure himself that, no, he had not suddenly gone deaf. He took out a cigarette, scraped a match noisily against the side of the box and lit it. He inhaled and exhaled as loudly as he could. The cigarette smoke drifted away undisturbed and, when the transport of Jumeau's breath had gone, it hung upon the still air, no sound to bounce the molecules around, no breeze from passing cabs to turn it inside out, no nothing but the weight of itself to slowly drag it to the ground, where it might remain like a low mist until the rains came to wash it away.

There was silence in the city.

It was strange how, after all these years of needing no one, Jumeau suddenly felt a panic surge through him. He might well have had no one, no one to call his own, but they were there, they were always there, leaning on their horns, slamming their doors, laughing, shouting, screaming and crying. They were *there*. If he chose to accept them, they were there. If he had wanted them, they were there.

He got out of the car and closed the door gently behind him with both hands so as to make no noise. To add to the noise that was already there was okay, but to rupture the silence seemed sinful. He glanced into the diner. The lights were on, reflected against the table tops and the chrome and the glasses, but there was no one. He walked to the door and pushed it open, entered, made for his usual stool at the counter, then walked past. He glanced at the kitchen. No one was cooking a thing. None one was there. He sniffed the air for Holly's perfume, for a hint of citrus and her natural pheromones and got nothing back, not even the smell of fried food and cigarettes.

He went behind the counter and looked back across the place. It was view he had never had before, like seeing the place you have lived your life for the first time from a hill. He leaned against the counter and pictured himself at his stool, 'the usual' in front of him, as he ate mechanically, joylessly, without tasting the food. He was a dog eating for the sake of eating. He would make sure to enjoy his food in future. When he had been with Holly, when he had talked to her that night, he had gloried in the burger and the fries. He could still taste the melted fat and the onions and the relish and the layer of golden oil upon the fries, could feel the satisfying bolus of food upon his tongue and feel the pleasure he got from swallowing it down and the ripe anticipation of the next mouthful. That was how it should always be. The last mouthful of food should be full of pleasurable regret, a deep sadness that this feast was almost over and that it would never be repeated, but that there would be a pleasure in the trying. He would make the effort in future. In future, he would share his mealtimes, fill the gap between mouthfuls with idle chatter and smiles and laughter, devour not just the food, but the companionship and the new knowledge that came with every new morsel of yakkety-yak. He had underestimated the power of yakkety-yak. He had isolated himself, shut himself off from the world for fear of repeating the hurt, little realising that it was the hurt that let you know you were alive, that the ups and the downs were what made the rollercoaster ride fun.

He scanned each table and chair and thought of all the people whose butts had shone those seats, the excited kids out on birthday treats, the lovers-to-be out on first dates, the tired and desperate on the verge of divorce, the passing through, truck drivers and businessmen and theatre-goers and shoppers on a money-high, friends full of gossip and enemies ready for reconciliation or the chance to descend further into hate, priests and police and refuse men and shop workers. The whole jamboree of life had passed through these doors and he had turned his back on it in favour of silent nourishment. In future, he would venture out, go to a table and say, *Is anybody sitting here? Mind if I join you? You look like you've been uptown and emptied just about every clothes store there is. What do you think to the burgers? Yes, they are juicy aren't they and the fries are just the right side of brown. They crunch when you bite down on them. Where are you from anyhow?* And from there he would make a friend for ten minutes or for a lifetime but, either way, he would make a friend.

That was his resolution, his pledge. It was no bargain with God or the Devil; it was just his word, given to himself in the silence of the diner, in the silence of the city, on this strangest of nights.

He moved out from behind the counter. There was unlikely to be anything going on in the diner for a while. He would go. He would go outside and take a tour of the silence, stick his hands in his pockets and walk the empty streets. So he did. He closed the door to the diner gently and stood on the sidewalk and looked both ways. He started to go left then hesitated and looked across the street. There was the jazz-joint. He had always wanted to go in there, walk into the calm, dimly lit heaven that was filled with that sweet smell of joints and liquor and the sweat of a hundred bodies shifting in their seats as they succumbed to the irresistible force of the trumpet and the sax and the piano and the deep throb of the bass and somewhere at the back the itchy fingers and paradiddles of a drummer who, with brushes or sticks and bouncing feet, shuffled through the tunes like the supple spine of an erotic dancer.

He would wait. That would be his reward. He would take himself where he had not been in years, past the boundary of the diner and the liquor store and into unknown territory, always with the thought that tonight of all nights he was safe, that he could climb over that wall and see the fields beyond.

He would have liked Wint to be here with him. He would have enjoyed the company. He thought that Wint was the kind of man that would have been happiest on the busy streets at night. He would have revelled in the lights, the neon above the doors, the skinny whores and drunks who rolled senseless and without care towards the next bar. He would have loved the smell of the exhausts and the permanent warm breeze that wheeled and eddied around the corners of alleyways and in the wake of the traffic. He would have basked in the torn jeans and raggedy filth and the high-heeled shoes and plush furs, the down-and-outs and the up-and-comings and the already-theres who mixed like the wrong colours on the palette yet came together on the canvas like a drop of Canaletto. He would have loved the XXX theatres with the coy posters of smiling women, lit from behind like fireflies in the hope of attracting money-mates, the surreptitious glances of men in suits hanging around the door trying to pluck up the courage to go in and touch the forbidden fruit with sweaty, shaky fingers and capsized hearts. He would have loved the department stores with their two hundred square feet of window dressing, the mannequins in hip-hugging skirts and busty summer tops, V-shaped dinner jackets and scarlet cummerbunds, the expensive mahogany tables beneath expensive candelabra and perfect plastic kids in their perfect American shirts and their tight-creased American pants with their white American smiles as they were stared at by toothless hobos and broken-down drunks and soft-bellied men and women with fat wallets and houses in The Valley. He would have loved the cinemas with the queues for Ben-Hur and Rio Bravo and North by Northwest,

Sleeping Beauty and Darby O'Gill, the smell of hotdogs and popcorn and the antsy-footed excitement of those waiting for a seat. He would have loved the tenements with the zigzag stairs that clung to the grimy outside walls and the thousand windows out of which came the sound of TVs and radios and shouts and laughter and singing. He would have loved the alleyways between them, with their litter and their garbage cans and their boxes that sometimes doubled as homes and the weak, yellow lights that permeated the darkness and seeped down the walls to land in a septic pool at the junction of building and ground. He would have loved the sidewalks carpeted by the moss of colour from all the windows and all the cars and all the lamps and all the stars. He would have loved it all, with his hands in his pockets, as he sauntered like a king though his realm of vice and faith and love and hate and thought himself a part of it all, a part of every building and passing car, every molecule of stardust that passed for human in this Godforsaken world.

This Godforsaken world. Forsaken by God. Created by God, who on the eighth day realised his mistake and averted his eyes and held up a hand in the hope that it would all go away. But it never did. It never did. From the churning, bubbling swamps and the misty humidity of the first elemental brew crawled the flippered, soft-spined life-form which

took a first breath of noxious air and survived. That
first brave step. That first brave breath. That first
brave human. The things that humankind had
achieved, all the greatness - the fire, the bridges, the
computers, the weapons, the architecture, the
medicines, the combustion engine, art, mathematics,
language, evolution and revolution - then the self-
mutilation and the decline into self-destruction.
How beautiful it had all been and somehow,
somewhere along the way, this artist, this
insignificant man, this upright fish, had lost his awe
and his ability to see the beauty and ended up reciting
from memory for the thrown pennies of the lucky
few. He had withdrawn from the world because he
was afraid. What foolish fear. Better to feel the quiver
of dread and shed tears at unattainable beauty than
suffer the dry regret and shame of underachievement
through reclusive self-control.

The city was indeed a beautiful beast, a living,
fire-breathing dragon that had become lost in the
science fiction droolings of twentieth century man.
It had colour, it had life, it had a heartbeat, as surely
as any forest or any meadow or any mountain range.
But it was not a forest or a meadow or a mountain
range, it was a man-made precipice from which man
would eventually tumble, to leave the forest to
encroach again upon the land from which it had been
banished so long ago, to leave the grass to grow

between the concrete cracks and the continents to rise again where man had flattened them with jackhammer and bulldozer.

He rounded a corner and found himself back in his street. He headed towards the jazz club and saw that, below the overhanging entrance, were the words *The Lounge* in bright pink neon, moulded into a refined hand, as if it was being mentioned in passing in a letter between friends. He had never realised that this was the name of the place. He had never been able to see the sign from the window of his room, only the pink glow of an unidentifiable something. When he had ventured outside, for his wine or to the diner, he had walked head-down, to avoid the eyes of others and the risk of contact, in any form.

Hands in pockets, he stood outside the club and lit a cigarette. The doors were brass framed and brass handled and within the frame was perfect glass, unscratched and unmarked. Beyond the doors was a red carpeted floor, lush as a lawn, which receded into an exciting dimness, beyond which lay paradise.

With a thrill in his heart, he walked through the doors and smelled the dope and the bourbon and the sweat and the perfume and the carpets and everything he had ever imagined he would smell if he ever plucked up the courage to cross that line.

16

Jumeau went to the bar. He had expected a *Mary Celeste* of a place, devoid of life, so he was pleasantly surprised to see someone behind the bar. He went up to the bar and raised himself up on a stool. The barman, who had been arranging glass bowls of nuts on the bar, looked at him with clear eyes and an unfurrowed brow. Jumeau liked him immediately. He was black, dressed in a white shirt which clung to his torso like a second skin, and black pants. Over the shirt he had the wildest vest Jumeau had ever seen, a madcap mix of shapes and colours that might actually have been the sound of jazz itself, thrown from a horn to land haphazard upon the first thing it found.

'Good evening, sir.' The barman placed his hands flat upon the bar. 'My name is George. What can I get you to drink?' George wasn't smiling, but his lips were parted enough to suggest that at any moment he might well do.

'Bourbon, please.' Jumeau held out his hand. 'My name is Jumeau.'

The barman shook his hand. 'Welcome, Mr Jumeau.'

'Just Jumeau.'

George nodded. 'As you wish, sir.'

From behind and to the left, Jumeau heard some shuffling footsteps reverberate in the shadows. A single spotlight came on and illuminated part of a stage, which was really a platform raised a foot off the ground, and in the light stood a man with a saxophone in his hand. He too was black, with a round face and soft, smiling eyes and behind all that lay a twitch of madness which, Jumeau knew, would any second electrify his fingers and pass like lightning into the sax. The man put his lips around the mouthpiece and blew silently, an embouchure that was as much technique as ritual, a silent genuflection to the icon in his hands, licked his lips, blew again, held the sax at a distance with his eyes closed, as if offering to the gods, then put the sax back in his mouth and stuttered into *Summertime*, all alone, no strings, no keys, no brushes in back, just him and his imagination.

Jumeau swivelled on the stool and gave the man his full attention. He could tell, he could just tell, that he was living in the tune, that outside of himself nothing existed but the air that carried away the notes. He had once felt the same about his art, that his brushes were just his fingers, that his eyes were a part of the canvas, that his brain was there only to transmit the glory of his thoughts, to translate the language of colour into something that others could understand. Right now, that sax player was doing the same, existing only for himself and his music, selfish to the needs of others, ostracising the so called civilised world in favour of the peaks and troughs of the bends and the tongue slaps, the growl at the back of his throat and the way his abdomen was rock hard as he forced his soul to rise from within and float free for others, if they so wished, to grasp and share.

The barman touched Jumeau's elbow to tell him that his bourbon was there. He raised a hand in thanks. He took out a Chesterfield and George was already there with a lit match.

'This guy's good,' said Jumeau. 'He sounds like Bird.'

George passed no comment, merely nodded and returned to polishing glasses not in any need of a polish.

'Why's it so quiet?' asked Jumeau.

'It won't be for long,' said George. 'People walk by, hear that sax or the trumpet or the piano and they just get naturally pulled our way. By the turn of midnight, we're usually fuller than a Titanic lifeboat with twice as much sway.'

As if his words had taken on a life of their own, people started to come through the door. And what a mix they were. First of all, the blacks came in, all cool, all balls of the feet, pleated pants around thin waists and sharp shirts that were not for wear but for display, hats laid lazy-style over one eye and constant back and forth between them until they heard the music and then they shut the hell up and almost tippy-toed to the bar. Their women wore low-slung purple or red or night-blue dresses, some with sea-blue stripes that ran like icy rivers towards the ground or polka dot and black that hugged their torsos, passed through a figure-loving belt at the waist and draped elegantly down over their knees. Some wore Medalo wigs that gave them that extra flick or a soft natural curl that their natural hair just did not deliver. They were beautiful and full of life and outshone their peacock men just by the grace of their being. They were followed by the whites; ladies in fox furs, long dresses that hugged at the hips and fell like silken waterfalls to the ground, and high heels that flattened their behinds and made their calves curve the right side of sexy, men in penguin suits and sharp imported suits. It was going to get as hot as hell in here if they kept coming in at this pace.

Jumeau decided to move to a table at the front before the place began to fill up too much and he got stuck at the bar. He leaned over to the barman.

'George, I'm going to sit over there. Would you be kind enough to keep an eye on my glass and, if you see it's empty, replace it with one full to the brim?'

I will, sir, I will.' He glanced at Jumeau's glass. 'Perhaps we should start now.'

Jumeau smiled and emptied the glass, then moved on over to the table he wanted. It was but two yards from the stage. The sound of the sax filled the place, its focal point the centre of the stage from where it simply oozed into every crack and crevice of the room and ran free beneath the tables and between the chairs until it found an ear in which to rest. It was smooth and mellow one moment, then cracking like a whip the next and taking the people and their humours with it, raising the room and then bringing it down like a dose of medication.

George kept his word and brought over a large glass of bourbon. He laid it without fuss on the table then retreated to the bar.

By the time the sax player was through with his fifth piece, *The Lounge* heaved at the seams. Everybody was having the time of their lives. Everybody was there for the bourbon and the sweet cigarettes and the music and to shun the restrictions forced upon them by the outside world. There was no black, no white, no rich, no poor, no with, no without, no man, no woman, no better, no worse, no praise, no condemnation, there was just being, being in the now, because the now was all. The sax player sweated like he was melting. Soon he would be a puddle in the spotlight into which people would dip their fingers and anoint themselves. He wound up the tune with a ferocity and deftness that mingled heaven and hell then held the final note as the room held its breath with him and was about to expire when he let go and they all breathed again.

'Taking five,' he said breathlessly into the microphone. The spot remained on, but was now empty save the yellow light that filled the saxophonist's place.

He stepped down from the stage, weary but high, a handkerchief in his hand as it wiped away at his face. He headed straight for Jumeau. 'May I sit here? It's close to the stage and means I don't have to walk far when it's time to get back up there.' He laughed heartily. 'I am a profoundly lazy man and will avoid effort at all costs.' He held out is hand. 'My name is Charlie.'

Jumeau took the hand. 'Jumeau. Please, sit.'

Charlie sat. 'Jumeau, eh? A man with a single handle. That's an equaliser. I like it.'

'It's easier that way, that's all.'

'I can appreciate that.' George brought Charlie over two drinks and laid them before him. Charlie thanked him. 'I like to have two drinks on my five; one to quench my thirst and the other to quench the fire.'

'You're good, Charlie. Really good.' Jumeau didn't want to come over all marshmallow-eyed, but he recognized the value of what Charlie had done and wanted him to know it.

Charlie put the first drink to sleep with a single swallow. 'I appreciate that. Is that one artist speaking to another or just a man with a hard-on for the moment?'

Jumeau smiled at Charlie's directness. 'Both. I paint, so I appreciate what you do. But I love jazz. I love bebop. It's Jackson Pollock and the madness of Magritte and the wanderings of Kandinsky, even Turner in his more abstract wanderings. Sometimes you have to lash yourself to the mast, you know?' Charlie rested his chin in his hand and nodded. 'I like things that break away into the abstract. We can always return to the safe, but it's an adventure to walk the tightrope.'

'I hear you,' said Charlie. 'If I had to do that nine to five shit, I would end up in the asylum. If I had to play the same note twice in a row it would send me deranged.' He leaned forward confidentially. 'You know, this music pretty much cost me everything - wife, home, kids, regular income, my liver, but it never cost me hope. It never, ever cost me hope because it was the only hope I ever had. When I blow that horn, I ain't simply reciting. No, sir. When I blow that horn, I'm living. I am giving out my soul in sound. The writer, he does it in words, the artist, he does in paints and the poet twists those words and feelings until they are tortured lovers who just did what their mama told them never to do. And you know what? I make no apologies. I've had my guilt, I've had my burdens, I've had my heartbreaks and losses, I've loved God and cursed his name, but that's what made me and I feel good about that because, in between, I have lived the life, I have picked the blossom from that tree, I *have* loved, I *have* lived free of guilt, I *have* done the best I can with my faulty wiring and I *have* made a difference to every living being I ever met, for good or bad. And then so have they. And then so have the people that they met. And then the ones that they met. Damn, I started off a whole chain reaction of my own and the world is a different place for all that.' He dug in his pocket and took out a joint the size of his thumb. He held it up to Jumeau. 'Do you mind if I do?' Jumeau shook his head. Charlie stuck the joint between his lips and lit it. He offered it to Jumeau, who declined. 'You feel the same, Jumeau?'

'I do,' said Jumeau. 'But I never saw it until now. No, that's not true. I lost it.'

'You found it again?'

'Yes.'

'Damn,' said Charlie with deep satisfaction. 'There I go again, starting off a whole new chain reaction. I am on fire.' He dragged deeply on the joint, held it inside his lungs until it burned, then let the smoke drift slowly from his nostrils as if he was releasing a troubled part of himself back into the wild. 'Do you play?' he asked.

'Play?'

'An instrument?'

'Me?' Jumeau laughed. 'No.' He shook his head and lit a cigarette.

'You sure? You look like a player to me. Show me your hands.' Jumeau held his hands up, spread like claws. 'Look at them things. Ten feet long and skinnier than my first wife. They, sir, are the fingers of a piano man. Look at that one, all bent and made for breaking away from the others to add in that extra beat. I bet that's a favourite with the ladies. Why, I bet you if you took a toke of this, you'd be up there with Jimmy Smith, stroking those keys like you were born to it.'

'I tried once,' said Jumeau a little sadly. 'I tried to play a friend's piano.'

'And?'

'I think I killed it.'

Charlie barked with laughter. 'No such thing! No, sir. No such thing ever happened. I saw your face when I was playing. You were playing every note along with me and others besides. You could hear that piano, grinding along and chipping in when my plumbing took a breath. Yes, I saw you. All these people,' he waved a hand around the room, 'I'm not saying that they don't appreciate the music, but they are here for the scene. You? You're here for the tunes. I know it and you know it. Deny that if you can.'

'I don't deny it,' said Jumeau. 'It's like being caught at the Louvre and trying to say you were only there for the comfortable benches. However, I cannot play the piano.'

'Would you try?'

Jumeau wondered just how strong Charlie's spliff really was. 'Here? Now?'

'Sure. Why not? It's jazz. People only get suspicious when you start playing the right notes. All you have to do is put your fingers on the keys and press. You've seen it a thousand times and heard it more.'

Jumeau looked suspiciously at Charlie. He couldn't be serious, could he? And yet he had all the conviction of a hanging judge who looked forward to his work. He shrugged. 'Sure. Why not?'

Charlie's face split into a wide grin. 'That's the spirit.' He drained his second drink, fizzed out the end of his joint with a wet finger, put it in his pocket and stood. 'Let's go and make some tunes,' he said.

'Christ!' cursed Jumeau beneath his breath. And yet, beneath the terror, he felt a buzz. How bad could it be? How difficult could it be? He had done this in his dreams so often and woken up so disappointed that it wasn't real that he would be a fool to turn it down now.

He crushed out his cigarette and followed Charlie to the stage. The gathering applauded spontaneously as they saw Charlie climb the single step into the sharp edge of the spotlight. Another spotlight came on and revealed a Steinway, black and shining, the lid open, its white teeth beaming like Charlie's smile.

Charlie picked up his sax and wrapped the strap around his neck. He went to the mic and waited for the crowd's clapping to die down.

Jumeau lowered himself onto the stool in front of the piano and put his feet on the pedals. He laid his hands on a middle C and pressed. The chord reverberated through the belly of the piano and spread like spilled wine in to the room. The onlookers lapped it up.

'This here,' said Charlie as he pointed a finger across at the piano, 'is a friend of mine called Jumeau. He is an artist and a man of the world. He loves jazz and bebop and he feels it. He doesn't just listen to it, he lives it, and even though he's an artist of the canvas rather than the note and doesn't play the box for a living, I know that he will move you to your core because he knows that all that matters is the art and all that matters is the now.' He put the sax to his lips and gave it another soundless blow, then looked across at Jumeau and nodded.

Jumeau looked at the man in the spot. He was a giant, with his hunched shoulders and his shining wet skin and his fingers flattened and spread through so many years of pressing the keys, and he had that keen madness back in his eyes as he prepared to hop from one dimension to another and to take his new friend with him. Jumeau nodded back and felt the butterflies of fear take flight within but, instead of tearing him down with the heavy weight of their trembling wings, they lifted him up, carried him away, boosted him towards that same other dimension through which he could see Charlie slide even as he blew out his cheeks and growled low in his throat and brought the horn to life. Jumeau brought his hands down with absolute certainty of their truth and then, as he felt the strings kick and the piano resound, he felt his notes float free and join Charlie's free notes in perfect unison on the air between them. He could almost see the colours of the sounds as they collided in mid-air and exploded into a powder of new sound, which drifted onward towards the audience, who were swaying and rolling and cheering and breathing in the coloured powders so that it got into their bloodstreams and fed their souls. He hammered away at the keys, improvising, a step ahead of Charlie, sometimes a step behind, but always knowing where he was, where he should be, while his fingers skittled like spiders across the ivory and came to rest where it seemed right to come to a rest, while his feet pressed down on the pedals and brought about a sublime sustain that lingered into the next note and fed into the notes that Charlie hung out long and hard upon the air. Then Charlie stepped over to him and they locked eyes and everything, but everything - their fingers, tongues, arms, hips, brains and nerves - started on towards the crescendo that was bound to come, that waited upon the musical horizon, for the two storm-fronts to collide and light up the sky with a fantastic mania that could only come from two people locked in a symbiosis of love and life and thought and deed.

And so they did.

And the whole room went silent for a moment as it held its breath, unbelieving of what they had just heard, of the jarring tenderness and the brutal beauty that they had just witnessed on a stage just a foot higher than them and just a few feet away. Then they cheered and they whooped and they shouted for more, more, more and wondered who that man, that artist, was that had come up onto the stage and sent a ripple through their lives.

Jumeau closed the lid, stood and shook Charlie's hand. 'There's no boundary,' shouted Charlie above the noise. 'Do you see?' His excitement shuddered through him and passed into Jumeau.

'I didn't know I could do that,' said Jumeau. 'I had no idea...'

'Yes, you did. You always did. Don't you see? There's no boundary line to art. All you need is the will.'

Charlie put a hand behind Jumeau's head and pulled him towards him. Their foreheads touched and they became brothers forever and some of the sweat that rolled down their faces was indeed tears for they had never felt such joy and knew they never would again.

They slowly separated and Jumeau left the stage. He was elated. He had never known such ecstasy, the ecstasy that he had strived for all his life, that he had searched for in each stroke of the brush, in each mixed palette, in each small creation upon the greater whole - the single strand of hair, the disarranged leaf, the snowflake that broke away and sat upon the shoulder of a stranger and drew the eye to that stranger's lined and lived-in face- that same ecstasy that contained all his hope and pushed him on and on and on. And now he knew that anything was possible, that he could paint with the best of them, in his own way, in his own style, with his own freedom, and not be accountable to the ghosts and the titans that restrained him. If only he had known all this so long ago and not shut himself off from the world afraid, not to compete, but to partake without ego or awe and to realise that his dream was not the dream of all but that this truth did not make it any less.

He returned to his seat and as he did so he noticed that at his table there was a girl, a girl with short blond hair and blue diamond eyes and she wore a dress of white with flowers of dark purple and red and leaves of dark green that threaded through the flowers on sinuous vines, and she was whole and beautiful and her name was Eidolon.

She smiled and held out her hand and he took it. Her skin was soft, her hand warm. She stood and drew him through the crowd, which parted and watched him pass.

Behind him, the Bird played with all his heart.

Where she was taking him he could not say, but he wanted to go, it was time to go, to move on and lay content with her below heavenly stars.

17

The knocking persisted. It was forceful, done by the fist of a man who had done this too often before. It was full of rat-a-tat-tat impatience, demanding, menacing, without compromise.

The knocking stopped, there was a muffled muttering and then a key could be heard to turn in the door. The old lock rolled and clicked and finally the mechanism, after a wiggle of the handle, slipped into place.

A large baggy man barged in past the landlady. 'Jesus Christ! It's like a goddam fridge in here. Oh, sweet Jesus would you look at that!'

The other man, slim-built and sharp-faced with a brown fedora that had seen better days and a crumpled suit that complemented the hat, ushered the landlady out of the room and said that they would find her downstairs if they needed her.

He closed the door behind the woman. His cold breath followed him as he turned his head to see what his partner had seen.

'Christ almighty! That him, Jim?'

'I guess so.'

'You want to search him?'

'No. Do you?'

'I'll flip you for it.' Al took a coin out of a hip pocket. 'Heads or tails.'

'Fuckoff, Al. I'm not doing that shit again. I always lose. You do it. I'm keeping my hands in my pockets. I'm too fucking cold. It's the beginning of February, for Christ's sake! Look at the goddam window.'

He went over to the open sash window. There was snow an inch deep inside on the sill. It was hard and the large crystals in it caught the grey light outside and flickered like dying bulbs. Nestled inside the snow was a tumbler. The snow inside the tumbler was slightly pink.

Al looked at the body. All it had on was a T-shirt and a pair of jeans. 'Skinny son-of-a-bitch,' he said. 'Not a big eater, I guess.' He took a grasp on the jeans and tried to turn the body over. 'Jesus,' he groaned. 'Jesus. He's stuck to the bed. He must've started decomposing and then froze up when this cold spell set in. How long since she last saw him?'

Jim kept his face to the window. He blew out a stream of icy breath and watched it disappear into nothing. 'A month she reckoned.'

'Yeah, well, he's good and glued. He'll have to be thawed out. Did she say his name?'

'Yeah. Something French, I think.'

'Makes a change from the home grown ones, I guess. I think we'll take her word for it this time, at least 'til he softens up in the morgue.' Al gave up on the body and looked at the bedside table. 'There you go. We have a syringe and a spoon and some matches. What's the matter with these people? Is it that they just don't want to live?'

Jim shrugged. 'I guess.'

Al narrowed his eyes at Jim. 'I love working with you, Jim, you know that? The way you chat and stuff? You brighten up my day.'

'Glad to hear it.' Jim wandered down the other end of the room. 'Christ, will you look at this. These guys call themselves artists? What the fuck is this supposed to be?' He reached out and picked up a canvas. 'What is this?' He peered closely. 'Is that a nuclear explosion? Look at these people! They're dissolving in the heat. Look at these kids' faces. They're melting. Sick bastard!' He tossed the canvas to the floor. Its frame fractured.

Al stood by an easel and contemplated another picture. 'Take a look at this. Must've been one of those modern artists, no soul and no talent, probably a pansy, too. What is that? A naked man? A monkey? A blob? What the fuck is he doing painting blobs?'

Jim stood next to him and took a look. 'I tell you that is just plain shit, whatever it is. Hey!' Jim brightened up. 'Look, a Dansette. My old lady wants one of those. He's got some Bird too and some of that classical stuff. He was a culture vulture.' He screwed his face up and rubbed the top of the record player with his hand. 'Asshole got paint on it.

Probably thought that was art too.' He unplugged the Dansette, picked up the machine and made for the door. 'Grab the LPs for me, will you, Al. There's bound to be few good ones in there. You know what amazes me, Al?'

'Many things, I would imagine, Jim.'

Jim ignored Al. 'That anyone like that could have the capacity to like jazz, let alone understand it.' Jim took a last disgusted look at the frozen corpse. 'What a fucking waste,' he said. 'Come on, let's get out of here. We've done our bit. We'll let the other suckers have him.'

Jim cradled the Dansette clumsily as he opened the door. Al picked up the LPs and tucked them under his arm.

'It's a tough job this sometimes, ain't it?' said Al as he pulled the door to.

Jim laughed as he reached the top of the dark stairway. 'Someone's got to do it. Might as well be us.'

The door closed quietly and the room fell silent again.

Outside a car horn flared and a hundred others joined in and the music of the city floated up through the open window.

Chris Bradbury is also the author of:

Mike Ward Adventures

The High Commissioner's Wife
The Devil Inside
Catfish
No Time to Repent
Semper Occultus
Epitaph

Mayflies
Eidolon
The Stilling of the Heart
The Ghost of Dormy Place and Other Tales
A Kind and Gentle Man
Praxis (Sci-Fi Fantasy - with Ian Makinson)
Praxis - Part Two: Regeneration Paradox (Sci-Fi Fantasy - with Ian Makinson)
Praxis - Part Three: The Liar's truth - (Sci-Fi Fantasy - with Ian Makinson)
Earthbound
Earthbound Part Two - Hellbound
Chine (Horror)
Uncomfortably Numb (Play)
The Scarlet Darter (fiction for children)
Unton's Teeth and Other Tales of Wordful Mystification (poems for children)

Phoenix - A Look at the Causes of World War Two
A Beginner's Guide to the Wars of the Roses
A Beginner's Guide to Creative Writing
A Beginner's Guide to Death

Printed in Great Britain
by Amazon

e143ea5a-fd73-4a8c-a9ea-057dde3cdaafR01